BARON TRUMP'S MARVELLOUS UNDERGROUND JOURNEY

BY

INGERSOLL LOCKWOOD

Published: 1893

Categories: Fantasy Fiction

ABOUT INGERSOLL LOCKWOOD

Lockwood became born in Ossining, New York, the son of Munson Ingersoll and Sarah Lewis (née Smith) Lockwood. Munson Lockwood, like his older brothers, Ralph and Albert, changed into a lawyer and intimate pal of Henry Clay. However, Munson typically done prominence as a army guy and civic activist. He became a general within the New York State Militia and commandant of its seventh Brigade. A exquisite admirer of the Hungarian statesman and freedom fighter Lajos Kossuth, Munson actively raised funds for him in New York. He became also one of the founders of

Ossining's first bank and Dale Cemetery and served as the Warden of Sing Sing jail from 1850 to 1855.

Like his father and uncles, Ingersoll Lockwood also educated as a attorney, even though his first function became as a diplomat. In 1862 he became appointed Consul to the Kingdom of Hanover by using Abraham Lincoln. At the time he was the youngest member of the USA consular force and served in that publish for four years. On his go back he established a legal practice in New York City along with his older brother Henry.By the Eighteen Eighties Lockwood had installed a parallel career as a lecturer and writer. In 1884, he married Winifred Wallace Tinker, a graduate of Vassar College and aspiring author. They had been divorced in 1892. That equal 12 months she married Edward R. Johnes, a lawyer by means of profession and a literateur by way of avocation. He become defined in Current Literature as Winifred's "type and maximum sympathetic literary advisor."

Lockwood spent his retirement years in Saratoga Springs, New York in which he published his last book, a group of poetry entitled In Varying Mood, or, Jetsam, Flotsam and Ligan in 1912. It opens with juxtaposed photos of Lockwood at age 35 and at age 70. In the preface, he wrote:The give up has nearly come. I'm simplest waiting for the signal to push off and start my voyage to the Isles of the Blest within the a ways Western Seas. I became troubled in my thoughts at first, for my little bark, staunch though it could be, sat too deep within the water. It changed into overladen with conceits that wouldn't be contemporary and merchandise that wouldn't be saleable in the Isles of the Blest. Overboard with it! Now that I even have lightened deliver I sense better.

Lockwood died in Saratoga Springs 5 years later at the age of 77.

CHAPTER I

BULGER IS GREATLY ANNOYED BY THE FAMILIARITY OF THE VILLAGE DOGS AND THE PRESUMPTION OF THE HOUSE CATS.—HIS HEALTH SUFFERS THEREBY, AND HE IMPLORES ME TO SET OUT ON MY TRAVELS AGAIN. I READILY CONSENT, FOR I HAD BEEN READING OF THE WORLD WITHIN A WORLD IN A MUSTY OLD MS. WRITTEN BY THE LEARNED DON FUM.— PARTING INTERVIEWS WITH THE ELDER BARON AND THE GRACIOUS BARONESS MY MOTHER.— PREPARATIONS FOR DEPARTURE.

Bulger was not himself at all, dear friends. There was a lack-lustre look in his eyes, and his tail responded with only a half-hearted wag when I spoke to him. I say half-hearted, for I always had a notion that the other end of Bulger's tail was fastened to his heart. His appetite, too, had gone down with his spirits; and he rarely did anything more than sniff at the dainty food which I set before him, although I tried to tempt him with fried chickens' livers and toasted cocks' combs—two of his favorite dishes.

There was evidently something on his mind, and yet it never occurred to me what that something was; for to be honest about it, it was something which of all things I never should have dreamed of finding there.

Possibly I might have discovered at an earlier day what it was all about, had it not been that just at this time I was very busy, too busy, in fact, to pay much attention to any one, even to my dear four-footed foster brother. As you may remember, dear friends, my brain is a very active one; and when once I become interested in a subject, Castle Trump itself might take fire and burn until the legs of my chair had become charred before I would hear the noise and confusion, or even smell the smoke.

It so happened at the time of Bulger's low spirits that the elder baron had, through the kindness of an old school friend, come into possession of a fifteenth-century manuscript from the pen of a no less celebrated thinker and philosopher than the learned Spaniard, Don Constantino Bartolomeo Strepholofidgeguaneriusfum, commonly known among scholars as Don Fum, entitled "A World within a World." In this work Don Fum advanced the wonderful theory that there is every reason to believe that the interior of our world is inhabited; that, as is well known, this vast earth ball is not solid, on the contrary, being in many places quite hollow; that ages and ages ago terrible disturbances had taken place on its surface and had driven the inhabitants to seek refuge in these vast underground chambers, so vast, in fact, as well to merit the name of "World within a World."

This book, with its crumpled, torn, and time-stained leaves exhaling the odors of vaulted crypt and worm-eaten chest, exercised a peculiar fascination upon me. All day long, and often far into the night, I sat poring over its musty and mildewed pages, quite forgetful of this surface world, and with the plummet of thought sounding these subterranean depths, and with the eye and ear of fancy visiting them, and gazing upon and listening to the dwellers therein.

While I would be thus engaged, Bulger's favorite position was on a quaintly embroidered leather cushion brought from the Orient by me on one of my journeys, and now placed on the end of my work-table nearest the window. From this point of vantage Bulger commanded a full view of the park and the terrace and of the drive leading up to the *porte-cochère*. Nothing escaped his watchful eye. Here he sat hour by hour, amusing himself by noting the comings and goings of all sorts of folk, from the hawkers of gewgaws to the noblest people in the shire. One day my attention was attracted by his suddenly leaping down from his cushion and giving a low growl of displeasure. I paid little heed to it, but to my surprise the next day about the same hour it occurred again.

My curiosity was now thoroughly aroused; and laying down Don Fum's musty manuscript, I hastened to the window to learn the cause of Bulger's irritation.

Lo, the secret was out! There stood half a dozen mongrel curs belonging to the tenantry of the baronial lands, looking up to the window, and by their barking and antics endeavoring to entice Bulger out for a romp. Dear friends, need I assure you that such familiarity was extremely distasteful to Bulger? Their impudence was just a little more than he could stand. Ringing my bell, I directed my servant to hunt them away. Whereupon Bulger consented to resume his seat by the window.

The next morning, just as I had settled myself down for a good long read, I was almost startled by Bulger bounding into the room with eyes flashing fire and teeth laid bare in anger. Laying hold of the skirt of my dressing-gown, he gave it quite a savage tug, which meant, "Put thy book aside, little master, and follow me."

I did so. He led me down-stairs across the hallway and into the dining-room, and then this new cause of discontent on his part became very apparent to me. There grouped around his silver breakfast plate sat an ancient tabby cat and four kittens, all calmly licking or lapping away at his breakfast. Looking up into my face, he uttered a sharp, complaining howl, as much as to say, "There, little master, look at that. Isn't that enough to roil the patience of a saint? Canst thou wonder that I am not happy with all these disagreeable things happening to me? I tell thee, little master, it is too much for flesh and blood to put up with."

And I thought so too, and did all in my power to comfort my unhappy little friend; but judge of my surprise upon reaching my room and directing him to take his place on his cushion, to see him refuse to obey.

It was something extraordinary, and set me to thinking. He noticed this and gave a joyful bark, then dashed into my sleeping apartment. He was gone for several moments, and then returned bearing in his mouth a pair of Oriental shoes which he laid at my feet. Again and again he disappeared, coming back each time with some article of clothing in his mouth. In a few moments he had laid a complete Oriental costume on the floor before my eyes; and would you believe me, dear friends, it was the identical suit which I had worn on my last travels in far-away lands, when he and I had been wrecked on the Island of Gogulah, the land of the Round Bodies. What did it all mean? Why, this, to be sure:—

"Little master, canst thou not understand thy dear Bulger? He is weary of this dull and spiritless existence. He is tired of this increasing familiarity on the part of these mongrel curs of the neighborhood and of the audacity of these kitchen tabbies and their families. He implores thee to break away from this life of revery and inaction, and for the honor of the Trumps to be up and away again." Stooping down and winding my arms around my dear Bulger, I cried out,—

"Yes, I understand thee now, faithful companion; and I promise thee that before this moon has filled her horns we shall once more turn our backs on Castle Trump, up and away in search of the portals to Don Fum's World within a

World." Upon hearing these words, Bulger broke out into the wildest, maddest barking, bounding hither and thither as if the very spirit of mischief had suddenly nestled in his heart. In the midst of these mad gambols a low rap on my chamber door caused me to call out,—

"Peace, peace, good Bulger, some one knocks. Peace, I say."

It was the elder baron. With sombre mien and stately tread he advanced and took a seat beside me on the canopy.

"Welcome, honored father!" I exclaimed as I took his hand and raised it to my lips. "I was upon the very point of seeking thee out."

He smiled and then said,—

"Well, little baron, what thinkest thou of Don Fum's World within a World?"

"I think, my lord," was my reply, "that Don Fum is right: that such a world must exist; and with thy consent it is my intention to set out in search of its portals with all safe haste and as soon as my dear mother, the gracious baroness, may be able to bring her heart to part with me."

The elder baron was silent for a moment, and then added: "Little baron, much as thy mother and I shall dread to think of thy being again out from under the safe protection of this venerable roof, the moss-grown tiles of which have sheltered so many generations of the Trumps, yet must we not be selfish in this matter. Heaven forbid that such a thought should move our souls to stay thee! The honor of our family, thy fame as an explorer of strange lands in far-away corners of the globe, call unto us to be strong hearted. Therefore, my dear boy, make ready and go forth once more in search of new marvels. The learned Don Fum's chart will stand thee by like a safe and trusty counsellor. Remember, little baron, the motto of the

Trumps, Per Ardua ad Astra—the pathway to glory is strewn with pitfalls and dangers—but the comforting thought shall ever be mine, that when thy keen intelligence fails, Bulger's unerring instinct will be there to guide thee."

As I stooped to kiss the elder baron's hand, the gracious baroness entered the room.

Bulger hastened to raise himself upon his hind legs and lick her hand in token of respectful greeting. The tears were pressing hard against her eyelids, but she kept them back, and encircling my neck with her loving arms, she pressed many and many a kiss upon my cheeks and brow.

"I know what it all means, my dear son," she murmured with the saddest of smiles; "but it never shall be said that Gertrude Baroness von Trump stood in the way of her son adding new glories to the family 'scutcheon. Go, go, little baron, and Heaven bring thee safely back to our arms and to our hearts in its own good time."

At these words Bulger, who had been listening to the conversation with pricked-up ears and glistening eyes, gave one long howl of joy, and then springing into my lap, covered my face with kisses. This done, he vented his happiness in a string of earsplitting barks and a series of the maddest gambols. It was one of the happiest and proudest days of his life, for he felt that he had exerted considerable influence in screwing to the sticking-point my resolution to set out on my travels once again.

And now the patter of hurrying feet and the loud murmur of anxious voices resounded through the castle corridors, while inside and out ever and anon I could hear the cry now whispered and now outspoken,—

"The little baron is making ready to leave home again."

Bulger ran hither and thither, surveying everything, taking note of all the preparations, and I could hear his joyous bark ring out as some familiar article used by me on my former journeys was dragged from its hiding-place.

Twenty times a day my gentle mother came to my room to repeat some good counsel or reiterate some valuable caution. It seemed to me that I had never seen her so calm, so stately, so lovable.

She was very proud of my great name and so, in fact, were every man, woman, and child in the castle. Had I not gotten off as I did, I should have been literally killed with kindness and Bulger slain with sweet-cake.

CHAPTER II

DON FUM'S MYSTERIOUS DIRECTIONS.—BULGER AND I SET OUT FOR PETERSBURG, AND THENCE PROCEED TO ARCHANGEL.—THE STORY OF OUR JOURNEY AS FAR AS ILITCH ON THE ILITCH.—IVAN THE TEAMSTER.—HOW WE MADE OUR WAY NORTHWARD IN SEARCH OF THE PORTALS TO THE WORLD WITHIN A WORLD.—IVAN'S THREAT.—BULGER'S DISTRUST OF THE MAN AND OTHER THINGS.

According to the learned Don Fum's manuscript, the portals to the World within a World were situated somewhere in Northern Russia, possibly, so he thought, from all indications, somewhere on the westerly slope of the upper Urals. But the great thinker could not locate them with any accuracy. "The people will tell thee" was the mysterious phrase that occurred again and again on the mildewed pages of this wonderful writing. "The people will tell thee." Ah, but what people will be learned enough to tell me that? was the brain-racking question which I asked myself, sleeping and waking, at sunrise, at high noon, and at sunset; at the crowing of the cock, and in the silent hours of the night.

"The people will tell thee," said learned Don Fum.

"Ah, but what people will tell me where to find the portals to the World within a World?"

Hitherto on my travels I had made choice of a semi-Oriental garb, both on account of its picturesqueness and its lightness and warmth, but now as I was about to pass quite across Russia for a number of months, I resolved to don the Russian national costume; for speaking Russian fluently, as I did a score or more of languages living and dead, I would thus be enabled to come and go without everlastingly displaying my passport, or having my trains of thought constantly disturbed by inquisitive travelling companions—a very important thing to me, for my mind possessed the extraordinary power of working out automatically any task assigned to it by me, provided it was not suddenly thrown off its track by some ridiculous interruption. For instance, I was upon the very point one day of discovering perpetual motion, when the gracious baroness suddenly opened the door and asked me whether I had pared the nails of my great toes lately, as she had observed that I had worn holes in several pairs of my best stockings.

It was about the middle of February when I set out from the Castle Trump, and I journeyed night and day in order to reach Petersburg by the first of March, for I knew that the government trains would leave that city for the White Sea during the first week of that month. Bulger and I were both in the best of health and spirits, and the fatigue of the journey didn't tell upon us in the least. The moment I arrived at the Russian capital I applied to the emperor for permission to join one of the government trains, which was most graciously accorded. Our route lay almost directly to the northward for several days, at the end of which time we reached the shores of Lake Ladoga. This we crossed on the ice with our sledges, as a few days later we did Lake Onega. Thence by land again, we kept on our way until Onega Bay had been reached, crossing it, too, on the ice, and so reaching the station of the same name, where we halted for a day to give our horses a well-deserved rest.

From this point we proceeded in a straight line over the snow fields to Archangel, an important trading-post on the White Sea.

As this was the destination of the government train, I parted with its commandant after a few days' pleasant sojourn at the government house, and set out, attended only by my faithful Bulger and two servants, who had been assigned to me by the imperial commissioner.

DEPARTURE FROM CASTLE TRUMP.

My course now carried me up the River Dwina as far as Solvitchegodsk; thence I proceeded on my way over the frozen waters of the Witchegda River until we had reached the government post of Yarensk, and from here on we headed due East until our hardy little horses had dragged us into the picturesque village of Ilitch on the Ilitch. Here we were obliged to abandon our sledges, for the snows had disappeared like magic, uncovering long vistas of green fields, which in a few days the May sun dotted with flowers and sweet shrubs. At Ilitch I was obliged to relinquish from my service the two faithful government retainers who had accompanied me from Archangel, for they had now reached the most westerly point which they had been commissioned to visit. I had become very much attached to them, and so had Bulger, and after their departure we both felt as if we were now, for the first time, among strangers in a strange land; but I succeeded in engaging, as I thought, a trustworthy teamster, Ivan by name, who made a contract with me for a goodly wage to carry me a hundred miles farther north.

"But not another step farther, little baron!" said the fellow doggedly. I was now really at the foot hills of the Northern Urals, for the rocky crests and snow-clad peaks were in full sight.

I turned many a wistful look up toward the wild regions shut in by their sheer walls and parapets, shaggy and bristling with black pines, for a low, mysterious voice came a whispering in my inward ear that somewhere, ah, somewhere in that awful wilderness, I should one day come upon the portals of the World within a World! In spite of all I could do Bulger took a violent dislike to Ivan and Ivan to him; and if the bargain had not been made and the money paid over, I should have looked about me for another teamster. And yet it would have been a foolish thing to do, for Ivan had two excellent horses, as I saw at a glance, and, what's more, he took the best of care of them, at every post rubbing them until they were quite dry, and never thinking of his own supper until they had been watered and fed.

His tarantass, too, was quite new and solidly built and well furnished with soft blankets, all in all as comfortable as you can make a wagon which has no other springs than the two long wooden supports that reach from axle to axle. True, they were somewhat elastic; but I could notice that Bulger was not overfond of riding in this curious vehicle with its rattlety-bang gait up and down these mountain roads, and often asked permission to leap out and follow on foot.

At length Ivan reported everything in readiness for the start; and although I would have fain taken my departure from Ilitch on the Ilitch in as quiet a manner as possible, yet the whole village turned out to see us off—Ivan's family, father, mother, sisters, and brothers, wife and children, uncles and aunts and cousins by dozens alone making up people enough to stock a small town. They cheered and waved their kerchiefs, Bulger barked, and I smiled and raised my cap with all the dignity of a Trump. And so we got away at last from Ilitch on the Ilitch, Ivan on the box, and Bulger and I at the back, sitting close together like two brothers that we were—two breasts with but a single heart-beat and two brains busy with the same thought—that come perils or come sudden attacks, come covert danger or bold and open-faced onslaught, we should stand together and fall together! Many and many a time as Ivan's horses went crawling up the long stretches of mountain road and I lay stretched upon the broad-cushioned seat of the tarantass with a blanket rolled up for a pillow, I would find myself unconsciously repeating those mysterious words of Don Fum:—

"The people will tell thee! The people will tell thee!"

So steep were the roads that some days we would not make more than five miles, and on others a halt of several hours would have to be made to enable Ivan to tighten his horses' shoes, grease the axles, or do some needful thing in or about his wagon. It was slow work, ay, it was very slow and tedious, but what matters it how many or great the difficulties, to a man who has made up his mind to accomplish a certain task? Do the storks or the wild geese stop to count the thousands of miles between them and their far-away homes when the time comes to turn their heads southward? Do the brown ants pause to count the hundreds of thousands of grains of sand which they must carry through their long corridors and winding passages before they have burrowed deep enough to escape the frost of midwinter?

There had been many Trumps, but never one that had thrown up his arms and cried, "I surrender!" and should I be the first to do it? "Never! Not even if it meant never to see dear old Castle Trump again!"

One morning as we went zigzagging up a particularly nasty bit of mountain road, Ivan suddenly wheeled about and without even taking off his hat, cried out,—

"Little baron, I cover the last mile of the hundred to-day. If thou wouldst go any farther north thou must hire thee another teamster; dost hear?"

"Silence!" said I sternly, for the fellow had broken in upon a very important train of thought.

Bulger, too, resented the man's insolence, and growled and showed his teeth.

"But, little baron, listen to reason," he continued in a more respectful tone, removing his cap: "my people will expect me back. I promised my father—I'm a dutiful son—I—"

"Nay, nay, Ivan," I interrupted sharply, "curb that tongue of thine lest it harm thy soul. Know, then, that I spoke with thy father, and he promised me that thou shouldst go a second hundred miles with me if need were, but on condition that I give thee double pay. It shall be done, and on top of that a goodly present for your *golubtchika* (darling)."

"Little baron, thou art a hard master," whimpered the man. "If the whim took thee thou wouldst bid me leap into the Giants' Well just to see whether it has a bottom or not. St. Nicholas, save me!"

"Nay, Ivan," said I kindly, "I know no such word as cruelty although I do confess that right seems harsh at times, but thou wert born to serve and I to command. Providence hath made thee poor and me rich. We need each other. Do thou thy duty, and thou wilt find me just and considerate. Disobey me, and thou wilt find that this short arm may be stretched from Ilitch to Petersburg."

Ivan turned pale at this hidden threat of mine; but I deemed it necessary to make it, for I as well as Bulger had scented treachery and rebellion about this boorish fellow, whose good trait was his love of his horses, and it has always been my rule in life to open my eyes wide to the good that there is in a man, and close them to his faults. But, in spite of kind words and kind treatment, Ivan grew surlier and moodier the moment we had passed the hundredth milestone.

Bulger watched him with a gaze so steady and thoughtful that the man fairly quailed before it. Hour by hour he became more and more restive, and upon leaving a roadside tavern, for the very first time since we had left

Ilitch on the Ilitch, I noticed that the fellow had been drinking too much *kwass*. He let loose his tongue, and raised his hand against his horses, which until that moment he had been wont to load down with caresses and pet names.

"Look out for that driver of thine, little baron," whispered the tavern-keeper. "He's in a reckless mood. He'd not pull up if the Giants' Well were gaping in front of him. St. Nicholas have thee in his safe keeping!"

CHAPTER III

IVAN MORE AND MORE TROUBLESOME.—BULGER WATCHES HIM CLOSELY.—HIS COWARDLY ATTACK UPON ME.—MY FAITHFUL BULGER TO THE RESCUE.—A DRIVER WORTH HAVING.—HOW I WAS CARRIED TO A PLACE OF SAFETY.—IN THE HANDS OF OLD YULIANA.—THE GIANTS' WELL.

When we halted for the night it was only by threatening the man with severe punishment upon my return to Ilitch that I could bring him to rub his horses dry and feed and water them properly; but I stood over him until he had done his work thoroughly, for I knew that no such horses could be had for love or money in that country, and if they should go lame from standing with wet coats in the chill night air, it might mean a week's delay.

Scarcely had I thrown myself on the hard mattress which the tavern-keeper called the best bed in the house, when I was aroused by loud and boisterous talking in the next room. Ivan was drinking and quarrelling with the villagers. I strode into the room with the arrows of indignation shooting from my eyes, and the faithful Bulger close at my heels.

The moment Ivan set eyes upon us he shrank away, half in earnest and half in jest, and called out,—

"Hey, look at the *mazuntchick*! [Little Dandy!] How smart he looks! He frightens me! See his eyes, how they shine in the dark! Look at the little demon on four legs beside him! Save me, brothers! Save me—he will throw me down into the Giants' Well! Marianka will never see me again! Never! Save me, brothers!"

"Peace, fellow," I called out sternly. "How darest thou exercise thy dull wit on thy master? Get thee to bed at once, or I'll have thee whipped by the village constable for thy drunkenness."

Ivan clambered up upon the top of the bake oven, and stretched himself out on a sheepskin; then turning to the tavern-keeper, I forbade him under any pretext whatever to give my servant any more liquor to drink. "*Akh, Vasha prevoskhoditelstvo* [Ah, your Excellency!]" exclaimed the tavern-keeper with a gesture of disgust, "the fools never know when they have had enough. It matters not what the tavern-keeper may say to them. They tell us not to spoil our own trade. *Akh!* [Ah!] they don't know when to stop. They have throats as deep as the 'Giants' Well!'"

"The Giants' Well! The Giants' Well!" I murmured to myself, as I again threw myself down upon the bag of hay which did service as a mattress for those who could afford to pay for it. It's strange how those words seem to be in every peasant's mouth, but I thought no more about it at that time. Sleep got the better of me, and with my usual good-night to the elder baron and the gracious baroness, my mother, I dropped off into sweet forgetfulness.

It is a good thing that I had the power of falling asleep almost at will, for with my restless brain ever throbbing and pulsating with its own over-abundance of strength, ever tapping at the thin panels of bone which covered it, like an imprisoned inventor pounding on his cell door and pleading to be let out into the daylight with his plans and schemes, I should simply have become a lunatic.

As it was, with the mere power of thought I ordered sweet slumber to come to my rescue, and so obedient was this good angel of mine, that all I had to do was simply to set the time when I wished to awaken, and the thing was done to the very minute.

As for Bulger, I never pretended to lay down any rules for him. He made it a practice of catching forty winks when he was persuaded that no danger of any kind threatened me, and even then, I am half inclined to believe that, like an anxious mother over her babe, he never quite closed both eyes at once.

Though entirely sobered by daybreak, yet Ivan went about the task of harnessing up with such an ill grace that I was obliged to reprove him several times before we had left the tavern yard. He was like a vicious but cowardly animal that quails before a strong and steady eye, but watches its opportunity to spring upon you when your back is turned.

I not only called Bulger's attention to the fellow's actions, and warned him to be very watchful, but I also took the precaution to examine the priming of the brace of Spanish pistols which I carried thrust into my belt.

We had scarcely pulled out into the highway when a low growl from Bulger aroused me from a fit of meditation; and this growl was followed by such an anxious whine from my four-footed brother, as he raised his speaking eyes to me, that I glanced hastily from one side of the road to the other.

Lo and behold! the treacherous Ivan was deliberately engaged in an attempt to overturn the tarantass and to get rid of his enforced task of transporting us any farther on our journey.

"Wretch!" I cried, springing up and laying my hand on his shoulder. "I perceive very plainly what thou hast in mind, but I warn thee most solemnly that if thou makest another attempt to overturn thy wagon, I'll slay thee where thou sittest."

For only answer and with a lightning-like quickness he struck a back-hand blow at me with the loaded end of his whipstock.

It took me full in the right temple, and sent me to the bottom of the tarantass like a piece of lead.

For an instant the terrible blow robbed me of my senses, but then I saw that the cowardly villain had turned in his seat and had swung the heavy handled whip aloft with intent to despatch me with a second and a surer blow.

Poor fool! he reckoned without his host; for with a shriek of rage, Bulger leaped at his throat like a stone from a catapult, and struck his teeth deep into the fellow's flesh.

He roared with agony and attempted to shake off this unexpected foe, but in vain.

By this time I had come to a full realizing sense of the terrible danger Bulger and I were both in, for Ivan had dropped his whip and was reaching for his sheath-knife.

But he never gripped it, for a well-aimed shot from one of my pistols struck him in the forearm, for I had no wish to take the man's life, and broke it.

The shock and the pain so paralyzed him that he fell over against the dashboard half in a faint, and then rolled completely out of the wagon, dragging Bulger with him. The horses now began to rear and plunge. I saw no more. There was a noise as of the roar of angry waters in my ears, and then the light of life went out of my eyes entirely. I had swooned dead away.

It seemed to me hours that I lay there on my back in the bottom of the tarantass with my head hanging over the side, but of course it was only minutes. I was aroused by a prickling sensation in my left cheek, and as I slowly came to myself I discovered that it proceeded from the gravel thrown up against it by one of the front wheels of the tarantass, for the horses were galloping along at the top of their speed, and there on the driver's seat sat my faithful Bulger, the reins in his teeth, bracing himself so as to keep them taut over the horses' backs; and as I sat up and pressed my hand against my poor hurt head, the whole truth broke upon me:—

The moment Ivan had struck the ground Bulger had released his hold upon the fellow's throat, and ere he had had a chance to revive had leaped up into the driver's seat, and, catching up the reins in his teeth, had drawn them taut and thus put an end to the rearing and plunging of the frightened beasts and started them on their way, leaving the enraged Ivan brandishing his knife and uttering imprecations upon mine and Bulger's heads as he saw his horses and wagon disappear in the distance. Now was it that a mad shouting assailed my ears and I caught a glimpse of half a dozen peasants who, seeing this, as they thought, empty tarantass come nearer and nearer with its galloping horses, had abandoned their work and rushed out to intercept it.

Judge of their amazement, dear friends, as their eyes fell upon the calm and skilful driver bracing himself on the front seat, and with oft repeated backward tosses of his head urging those horses to bear his beloved master farther and farther away from the treacherous Ivan's sheath-knife.

As the peasants seized the animals by the heads and brought them to a standstill, I staggered to my feet, and threw my arms around my dear Bulger. He was more than pleased with what he had done, and licked my bruised brow with many a piteous moan.

"St. Nicholas, save us!" cried one of the peasants, devoutly making the sign of the cross; "but if I should live long enough to fill the Giants' Well with pebbles, I never would expect to see the like of this again."

"The Giants' Well, the Giants' Well!" I murmured to myself as I followed one of the peasants to his cot, standing a little back from the highway, for I stood sore in need of rest after the terrible experience I had just had. The blow of Ivan's whip-handle had jarred my brain, and I was skilled enough in surgery to know that the hurt called for immediate attention. As good luck would have it, I found beneath the peasant's roof one of those old women, half witches perhaps, who have recipes for everything and who know an herb for every ailment. After she had examined the cut made by the loaded whip-handle, she muttered out,—

"It is not as broad as the mountain, nor as deep as the Giants' Well, but it's bad enough, little master."

"The Giants' Well again," thought I, as I laid me down on the best bed they could make up for me. "I wonder where it may be, that Giants' Well, and how deep it is, and who drinks the water that is drawn from it?"

CHAPTER IV

MY WOUND HEALS.—YULIANA TALKS ABOUT THE GIANTS' WELL.—I RESOLVE TO VISIT IT.—PREPARATIONS TO ASCEND THE MOUNTAINS.—WHAT HAPPENED TO YULIANA AND TO ME.—REFLECTION AND THEN ACTION.—HOW I CONTRIVED TO CONTINUE THE ASCENT WITHOUT YULIANA FOR A GUIDE.

It was a day or so before I could walk steadily, and meantime I made unusual efforts to keep my brain quiet, but in spite of all I could do every mention of the Giants' Well by one of the peasants sent a strange thrill through me, and I would find myself suddenly pacing up and down the floor, and repeating over and over again the words, "Giants' Well! Giants' Well!"

Bulger was greatly troubled in his mind, and sat watching me with a most bewildered look in his loving eyes. He had half a suspicion, I think, that that cruel blow from Ivan's whip-handle had injured my reasoning powers, for at times he uttered a low, plaintive whine. The moment I took notice of him, however, and acted more like myself, he gamboled about me in the wildest delight. As I had directed the peasants to drive Ivan's horses back towards Ilitch on the Ilitch, until they should meet that miscreant and deliver them to him, I was now without any means of continuing my journey northward, unless I set out, like many of my famous predecessors, on foot. They had longer legs than I, however, and were not loaded with so heavy a brain in proportion to their size, and a brain, too, that scarcely ever slept, at least not soundly. I was too impatient to reach the portals to the World within a World to go trudging along a dusty highway. I must have horses and another tarantass, or at least a peasant's cart. I must push on. My head was quite healed now, and my fever gone.

"Hearken, little master," whispered Yuliana; such was the name of the old woman who had taken care of me, "thou art not what thou seemst. I never saw the like of thee before. If thou wouldst, I believe thou couldst tell me how high the sky is, how thick through the mountains are, and how deep the Giants' Well is."

I smiled, and then I said,—

"Didst ever drink from the Giants' Well, Yuliana?"

At which she wagged her head and sent forth a low chuckle.

"Hearken, little master," she then whispered, coming close to me, and holding up one of her long, bony fingers, "thou canst not trick me—thou knowest that the Giants' Well hath no bottom."

"No bottom?" I repeated breathlessly, as Don Fum's mysterious words, "The people will tell thee!" flashed through my mind. "No bottom, Yuliana?"

"Not unless thine eyes are better than mine, little master," she murmured, nodding her head slowly.

"Listen, Yuliana," I burst out impetuously, "where is this bottomless well? Thou shalt lead me to it; I must see it. Come, let's start at once. Thou shalt be well paid for thy pains."

"Nay, nay, little master, not so fast," she replied. "It's far up the mountains. The way is steep and rugged, the paths are narrow and winding, a false step might mean instant death, were there not some strong hand to save thee. Give up such a mad thought as ever getting there, except it be on the stout shoulders of some mountaineer."

"Ah, good woman," was my reply, "thou hast just said that I am not what I seem, and thou saidst truly. Know, then, thou seest before thee the world-renowned traveller, Wilhelm Heinrich Sebastian von Troomp, commonly called 'Little Baron Trump,' that though short of stature and frail of limb, yet what there is of me is of iron. There, Yuliana, there's gold for thee; now lead the way to the Giants' Well."

"Gently, gently, little baron," almost whispered the old peasant woman, as her shrivelled hand closed upon the gold piece. "I have not told thee all. For leagues about, I ween, no living being excepting me knows where the Giants' Well is. Ask them and they'll say, "It's up yonder in the mountains, away up under the eaves of the sky." That's all. That's all they can tell thee. But, little master, I know where it is, and the very herb that cured thy hurt head and saved thee from certain death by cooling thy blood, was plucked by me from the brink of the well!" These words sent a thrill of joy through me, for now I felt that I was on the right road, that the words of the great master of all masters, Don Fum, had come true.

"The people will tell thee!"

Ay, the people had told me, for now there was not the faintest shadow of doubt in my mind that I had found the portals to the World within a World! Yuliana should be my guide. She knew how to thread her way up the narrow pass, to turn aside from overhanging rocks which a mere touch might topple over, to find the steps which nature had hewn in the sides of the rocky parapets, and to pursue her way safely through clefts and gorges, even the entrance to which might be invisible to ordinary eyes. However, in order that the superstitious peasants might be kept friendly to me, I gave it out that I was about to betake myself to the mountains in search of curiosities for my cabinet, and begged them to furnish me with ropes and tackle, with two good stout fellows to carry it for me, promising generous payment for the services.

They made haste to provide me with all I asked for, and we set out for the mountain path at daybreak. Yuliana, in order not to seem to be of the party, had gone on ahead by the light of the moon, telling her people that she wished to gather certain herbs before the sun's rays struck them and dried the healing dew that beaded their leaves.

ALONG A HIGHWAY OF THE UNDER WORLD.

All went well until the sun was well up over our heads, when suddenly I heard a woman, who proved to be Yuliana, utter a piercing scream. In a moment or so the mystery was solved. The old beldam came rushing down the mountain, her thin wisp of gray hair fluttering in the wind. Her hands were tied behind her, and two young peasants with birchen rods were beating her every chance they got.

"Turn back, turn back, brothers," they cried to my two men. "The little wizard there has struck hands with this old witch. They're on their way to the Giants' Well. They'll loosen a band of black spirits about our ears. We shall all be bewitched. Quick! Quick! Cast off the loads ye're bearing and follow us."

The two men didn't wait for a second bidding, and throwing the tackle on the ground, they all disappeared like a flash, but for several moments I could hear the screams of poor Yuliana as these young wretches beat the old woman with their birchen rods.

Well, dear readers, what say ye to this? Was I not in a pleasant position truly? Alone with Bulger in that wild and gloomy mountain region, the black rocks hanging like frowning giants and ogres over our heads, with the dwarf pines for hair, clumps of white moss for eyes, vast, gaping cracks for mouths, and gnarled and twisted roots for terrible fingers, ready to reach down for my poor little weazen frame.

Did I fall a-trembling? Did I make haste to follow those craven spirits down the mountain side? Did I shift the peg of my courage a single hole lower?

Not I. If I had I wouldn't have been worthy of the name I bore. What I did do was to throw myself at full length on a bed of moss, call Bulger to my side, and close my eyes to the outer world.

I have heard of great men going to bed at high noon to give themselves up to thought, and I had often done it myself before I had heard of their doing it.

In fifteen minutes, by nature's watch—the sun on the face of the mountain—I had solved the problem. Now, there were two difficulties staring me in the face; namely, to find somebody to show me the way up the mountain, and if that body couldn't carry my tackle, then to find somebody else who could.

It suddenly occurred to me that I had noticed some cattle grazing at the foot of the mountain, and, what's more, that these cattle wore very peculiar yokes.

"What are those yokes for?" I asked myself, for they were of a make quite different from any that I remembered ever having seen, and consisted of a stout wooden collar from the bottom of which there projected backward between the beast's forelegs a straight piece of wood armed with an iron spike pointing toward the ground. At the top the yoke was bound by a leather thong to the animal's horns. So long, therefore, as the beast held his head naturally or even lowered it to graze, the yoke was drawn forward and the hook was kept free from the ground, but the very moment the animal raised his head in the air, at once the hook was thrown into the ground and he was prevented from taking another step forward. Now, dear readers, you may or may not know that when a cleft-hoofed animal starts to ascend a steep bank, unlike a solid-hoofed beast, he throws his head into the air instead of lowering it, and therefore it struck me at once that the purpose of this yoke was to keep the cattle from making their way up the sides of the mountain and getting lost.

But why should they want to clamber up the mountain sides? Simply because there was some kind of grass or herbage growing up there which was a delicacy to them, and knowing, as I well did, what risks animals will take and what fatigue they will undergo to reach a favorite grazing-ground, it struck me at once that if I would make it possible for them to reach this favorite food of theirs, they would be very glad to give me a lift on my way.

No sooner said than done. I forthwith retraced my steps until I fell in with a group of these cattle; and it did not take me many minutes to loosen their yokes from their horns and tie the hooks up under their bodies so that their progress up hill would not be interfered with.

They were delighted to find themselves so unexpectedly freed from the hateful drawback which permitted them merely to view the coveted grazing-grounds from afar, and then having cut me a suitable goad, I again started up the mountain, driving my new friends leisurely on ahead of me.

Upon reaching the spot where the superstitious peasants had thrown the tackle to the ground, I proceeded to load it upon the back of the gentlest beast of the lot, and was soon on my way again.

CHAPTER V

UP AND STILL UP, AND THROUGH THE QUARRIES OF THE DEMONS.—HOW THE CATTLE KEPT THE TRAIL, AND HOW WE CAME AT LAST UPON THE BRINK OF THE GIANTS' WELL.—THE TERRACES ARE SAFELY PASSED.—BEGINNING OF THE DESCENT INTO THE WELL ITSELF.—ALL DIFFICULTIES OVERCOME.—WE REACH THE EDGE OF POLYPHEMUS' FUNNEL.

Generally speaking, people with very large heads are fitted out by nature with a pair of rather pipe-stemmy legs, but such was not my case. I was blest with legs of the sturdiest sort, and found no difficulty in keeping pace with my new four-footed friends who, to my delight, were not long in convincing me that they had been there before. Not for an instant did they halt at any fork in the path, but kept continually on the move, often passing over stretches of ground where there was no trail visible, but coming upon it again with unfailing accuracy. Once only they halted, and that was to slake their thirst at a mountain rill, Bulger and I following their example.

It was only too evident to me that they had in mind a certain grazing-ground, and were resolved to be satisfied with no other; so I let them have their own way, for, as it was still up, up, up, I felt that it was perfectly safe to follow their lead.

At last the mountain side began to take on quite another character. The gorges grew narrower, and at times overhanging rocks shut out the sunlight almost entirely. We were entering a region of peculiar wildness, of fantastic grandeur.

I had often read of what travellers termed the "Quarries of the Demons" in the Northern Urals, but never till now had I the faintest notion of what the expression meant.

Imagine to yourself the usual look of ruin and devastation around and about a quarry worked by human hands, then in your thoughts conceive every chip to be a block, and every block a mass; add four times its size to every slab and post and pediment, and then turn a mighty torrent through the place and roll and twist and lift them up in wild confusion, end on end and on each other piled, till these wild waters have built fantastic portals to temples more fantastic, and arched wild gorges with roofs of rock which seem to hang so lightly that a breath or footfall might bring them down with terrible crash, and then, dear friends, you may succeed in getting a faint idea of the wild and awful grandeur of the scene which now lay spread out before me.

Would the cattle that had now led Bulger and me so safely up the mountain side know where to find an entrance to this wilderness of broken rock, and what was more important still, would they, when once engaged within its winding courts and corridors, its darkened maze of wall and parapet, its streets and plazas roughly paved as if by demon hands impatient of the task, know how to find their way out again?

Dear friends, man has always been too distrustful of his four-footed companions. They have much that they might tell us had they but speech to tell it with. I have often trusted them when it would have seemed foolhardy to you, and never once have I had cause to repent of doing so.

So Bulger and I, with stout hearts, followed straight after these silent guides, although I must confess my legs were beginning to feel the terrible strain I had put them to; but I resolved to push on ahead, at least until we had cleared the Demons' Quarry, and then to bring my little herd to a halt and pass the rest of the day and the night season in well-earned repose.

Once within the quarry, however, all sense of fatigue vanished, and my thankful mind, entranced and fascinated by the deep silence, the awful grandeur, the mysterious lights and shadows of the place, lent me new strength. At length we had traversed this city of silence and gloom, and once again we emerged into the full glory of the afternoon sun.

Suddenly my little drove of cattle, with playful tossing of their heads, broke into a run, Bulger and I at their heels, however. It was a mad race; but, dear friends, when it ended I took off my fur cap and tossed it high into the air with a wild cry of joy, and Bulger broke out in a string of yelps and barks, for, look ye, the cattle were grazing away for dear life there in front of me, and as their breath reached me my keen nostrils recognized the odor of Yuliana's herbs which she had bound on my hurt head.

Yes, we stood almost upon the brink of the Giants' Well, but I was too tired to take another step farther, too tired, in fact, to eat, although I had a stock of dried fruit in my pockets, and noticed that the nests of the wild fowl were well supplied with eggs. Having unloosened the tackle from the back of the good beast that had carried it up the mountain for me, I threw myself on the ground and was soon fast asleep, with my faithful Bulger coiled up close against my breast.

In the morning the cattle were nowhere to be seen, but I didn't trouble myself about them, for I knew that old Yuliana would be sent up after them the moment they were missed. After a hearty breakfast on half a dozen roasted eggs of the wild fowl, with some dried fruit and wintergreen berries, Bulger and I advanced to the edge of the Giants' Well, or, rather, to the edge of the vast terraces of rock leading down to it, each of which was from thirty to fifty feet in sheer height.

Before I go any farther, dear friends, I must beg you to remember that I am an expert in the use of tackle, there being no knot, noose, or splice known to a sailor which I didn't have at my fingers' ends, a fact not to be wondered at when you take into consideration the thousands of miles which I have travelled on water.

Nor would I have you shake your heads and look only half persuaded when I go on describing our descent into the Giants' Well, for of course you'll be asking yourselves how I succeeded in getting the tackle down when there was no one left at the other end to untie it!

Know, then, that that was the smallest of my troubles; for, as any sailor will tell you, you only need to tie your line in what is known as a "fool's knot," to one end of which you make fast a mere cord. The moment you have reached the bottom, a sharp tug at the cord unties the fool's knot, and your tackle falls down after you. My method was to lower Bulger down first, and then let myself down after him. In this way we proceeded from parapet to parapet, until at last we stood upon the very edge of the vast well, the existence of which had been so mysteriously hinted at in Don Fum's manuscript. Its mouth was probably fifty feet in width, and by straining my eyes I satisfied myself of the existence of a shelf of rock on one side, as nearly as I could judge about seventy-five feet down. It was a goodly stretch, and would require every foot of my rope. You will not smile, I'm sure, when I tell you that I pressed Bulger to my breast, and kissed him fondly before lowering away. He returned my caresses, and by his joyous yelp gave me to understand that he had perfect faith in his little master.

In a few moments I had joined him on this narrow shelf of rock. Below us now was darkness, but think you I hesitated? I knew that my eyes would soon become accustomed to the gloom, and I also knew that when my eyes failed Bulger's keener ones were there to help me out.

I rigged my tackle now with extra care, for I was really lowering my little brother on a sort of trip of discovery.

He was soon out of sight, and then, in spite of my calmness, I drew a quick breath, and my heart started upward a barleycorn or so. But hark! his quick, sharp bark comes plainly up to me. It means that he has landed upon a safe shelf or ledge, and the next moment my legs encircled the rope, and I began to glide noiselessly down into the stilly depths, his glad voice ringing in my ears.

Again and again did I send my wise and watchful little brother down ahead of me, until at last, standing there and looking up, naught remained to me of the mighty outside world but a bright silver speck, like a tiny ray of light streaming through a pin-hole in the curtains of your chamber.

But stop, have we reached the bottom of the Giants' Well? for with a trial plummet I find that the walls are no longer sheer; they slope inward, and gently too, almost so much so that I hardly need a line to continue my descent. Lighting one of my little tapers, I make my way cautiously around the edge. In half an hour I find myself back at the starting-place. The curve to the path has been always the same, while my trial plummet at all times has indicated the same slope to the rocky basin. And then for the first time, two certain words made use of by that learned Master of

Masters, Don Fum, till then a mystery to me, stood out before my eyes as if written with a pen of fire upon those black walls thousands of feet below the great world of light which I had quitted a few hours before. Those words were Polyphemus' Funnel! Yes, there could be no doubt of it: I had reached the bottom of the Giants' Well. I stood upon the edge of Polyphemus' Funnel!

CHAPTER VI

MY DESPAIR UPON FINDING THE PIPE OF THE FUNNEL TOO SMALL FOR MY BODY.—A RAY OF HOPE BREAKS IN UPON ME.—FULL ACCOUNT OF HOW I SUCCEEDED IN ENTERING THE PIPE OF THE FUNNEL.—MY PASSAGE THROUGH IT.—BULGER'S TIMELY AID.—THE MARBLE HIGHWAY AND SOME CURIOUS THINGS CONCERNING THE ENTRANCE TO THE WORLD WITHIN A WORLD.

The rocky sides of Polyphemus' Funnel were apparently as well polished as those of any tin funnel that I had ever seen hanging in the kitchen of Castle Trump, so making fast my tackle and taking Bulger in my arms, away we went sliding down the side with the line passed under my arm for safety's sake.

It was nearly a hundred feet to the bottom, for I had measured off the full length of my line before I had come to the apex of this gigantic cone, and not caring to tumble headlong down its pipe, I proceeded to light a taper and look about me.

Ah, dear friends, I can feel that shudder now, so terrible was it, and what wonder, too, for a glance at the pipe of the funnel told me that it was too small to let my body pass through. The agonizing thought flashed through my mind that I had committed a terrible error—that I had mistaken some vast pit for the Giants' Well, that I had thrown Bulger's and my own life away in mad and unreasoning haste, that I should never reach the wonderful World within a World, that there in that thick gloom must we lay our bodies and bones.

Or, thought I, may not the learned Master of Masters, Don Fum, have made an error himself in holding out the idea that the pipe of Polyphemus' Funnel was large enough to admit the passage of a man's body?

In my almost frenzy I advanced to the mouth of the pipe, and, lowering myself into it, let my body sink as far as it would.

It caught at the shoulders, and after a careful examination I was forced to reach the brain-racking conclusion that my faithful Bulger and I had travelled our last mile together.

There was nothing for us to do but to lie down and die.

Lie down and die? Never! I had noticed in making the descent into the Giants' Well that its side had much the appearance of being walled around by blocks of stone. With Bulger strapped to my back I would slowly climb up from shelf to shelf until my strength failed me, and then I would wait until I thought old Yuliana had come back to gather herbs, and possibly I might make her hear me.

In my despair I sighed and clutched my own arms, and as I did so one of my hands came into contact with something cold and slippery having the feel of tallow. Taking a pinch of the substance between my thumb and finger, I rubbed it thoughtfully for a moment, and then a ray of hope broke through the awful gloom that enshrouded me so pitilessly. It was black lead—there could be no doubt of it. It had made its way through a crack or crevice in Polyphemus' Funnel, and I had rubbed it off in sliding down the side. With this greasy material to rub on the inside of the pipe to the funnel, and also to besmear myself with, mayhap I might yet slip through into the World within a World!

At any rate, I determined to make the trial, even if I left some of my skin on the flinty rock.

In order to collect my thoughts thoroughly, and that I might proceed step by step in that systematic order so characteristic of all my wonderful exploits, I sat down, and putting my arm around dear Bulger's neck and drawing him up against me, I communed with myself for a good half-hour.

BEFORE HER MAJESTY GALAXA, QUEEN OF THE MIKKAMENKIES.

Then all was in readiness for action; and to prove to you, dear friends, how careful Bulger was not to interrupt my train of thought, I have to report to you that although a small animal of the rat family came out from a crevice in the rock while I sat there thinking, as I could see by the light of my tiny wax taper, and had the temerity first to sniff at Bulger's tail and then to give it a playful nip, yet the sagacious animal never budged a hair's breadth.

"Mind hath ordered, now let hands obey!" I exclaimed, as I sprang up and began stripping off my outer garments. This done, I clambered up on the side of the funnel, and began to collect a supply of the black lead, which I deposited near the opening of the pipe. The next thing to do was to get Bulger through the pipe ahead of me. To this end I tied him up in my clothing, bag fashion, and began to lower away.

After paying out sixty-five or seventy feet of the line, he struck bottom, and by his loud barking gave me to understand that it was all right, that I might make the descent myself. Upon hearing his voice, I gave the line a few sharp tugs. He was not slow to comprehend my meaning, and in a moment or so had not only scrambled out of the bag himself, but pulled my clothing loose, so that I might draw the line up again.

My next step was to contrive a way to weight myself when the moment arrived to begin the descent, for I felt sure that I never should be able to arrange it so as to slip through the pipe unless something was pulling at my heels.

Cutting off about ten feet of the rope, I made fast one end of the piece to a long piece of rock, weighing about a hundred pounds. This I laid near the mouth of the pipe ready for use. But now came the most difficult thing of all—it was to draw my shoulders in on my breast and lash them securely in that position, by which plan I expected to reduce my width by at least two good inches.

These two inches thus gained, or, rather, lost, might be the means by which I would be able to slip through the pipe of Polyphemus' Funnel and reach the vast underground passage leading to the World within a World. Putting a noose around my chest, just below my collar bone, I drew my shoulders in as tight as I could bear, and changed the slip knot into a hard one; then having made the other end of the line fast to the side of the funnel, I proceeded to wind myself up as the housewives often do a big sausage to keep it from bursting. This done, I set about rolling in the black lead until I was thoroughly smeared with it.

There was now but one thing more to do before dropping myself into the pipe, and that was to make fast the weight to my feet. It was no easy task, wound up as I was, with my arms lashed down against my body, but by the use of slip knots I finally accomplished the feat, and sitting down put my legs into the pipe and drew a long breath, for I felt as if I was skewered up in a straight jacket.

Bending down, I called out to Bulger. He answered with a yelp of joy that brought fresh vigor to my heart. Now was come the supreme moment which was to witness success or failure. Failure! Oh, what a dread word is that! and yet how often must human lips pronounce it, and in so doing breathe out the sigh in which it ends! Quickly lowering the weight, I wriggled off the edge of the opening, and straightened myself out as I slipped into the pipe.

Had I stopped it like a cork, or was I moving? Yes, down, down, gently, slowly, noiselessly, I went slipping through the pipe to Polyphemus' Funnel. What did I care how that weight caused the line to cut into my ankles? I was moving, I was drawing nearer and nearer to Bulger, whose joyous bark I could hear now and then, nearer to the inner gates of the World within a World!

But woe is me! I suddenly stop, and in spite of all my efforts to start again by twisting, turning, and shaking my body, it refused to sink another inch, and there I stick.

"Oh, Bulger, Bulger," I moan, "faithful friend, if thou couldst but reach me, one tug from thee might save thy little master!"

In a sort of a wild and desperate way I now began to feel about me as well as I could with my hands wedged in so close to my sides, but in a moment or so I had discovered the cause of my coming to such a sudden standstill.

I had struck a portion of the pipe that had a thread to it, like that which encircles a bolt of iron and makes a screw of it, and the thought came to me that if I could only succeed in giving a revolving motion to my body, I would with every turn twist myself farther down toward the end of the pipe.

I could feel that my knuckles and finger tips were being bruised and lacerated by this arduous work, but what cared I for the keen pain that darted from hands to wrists, and wrists to elbows! It was like twisting a screw slowly through a long nut, only the thread in this case was on the nut and the grooves in the screw, and that screw was my poor bruised little body!

All of a sudden, by the swinging of the weight, I could tell that it had passed out at the lower end of the pipe. It was pulling cruelly hard on my tender ankles, but I could twist myself no more; my strength was gone. I was at the point of swooning when I heard Bulger utter a loud yelp, and the next instant there was such a strong tug at my ankles that I sent forth a groan, but that tug saved me! It was Bulger who had leaped into the air, and catching the rope in his teeth had dragged his little master out of the pipe of Polyphemus' Funnel!

We all fell into the same heap, Bulger, I, and the weight, fully ten feet, and very serious might have been the consequences for me had my fall not been broken by my striking on the pile of my clothing placed directly under the opening; and, dear friends, if you talked until the crack o' doom you could not make me believe that my four-footed brother hadn't placed those clothes there to catch me.

They weren't thrown higgledy-piggledy into a heap either, but were laid one upon the other, the heaviest at the bottom.

Having unwound myself and lighted one of my wax tapers, I made haste to cast away the undergarment with its coating of black lead and resume my clothing; then stooping down, I made an examination of the floor. It was composed of huge blocks of marble of various colors, polished almost as smooth as if the hand of man had wrought the work; and then I knew that I was on Nature's Marble Highway leading to the cities of the under world which Don Fum had mentioned in his book, and I remembered, too, that he had spoken of Nature's Mighty Mosaics, huge fantastic figures on the walls of these lofty corridors, made up of various colored blocks and fragments laid one upon the other as if with design, and not by the wild, tempestuous whims of upbursting forces thousands of years ago, when the earth was in its mad and wayward youth. After a rest of several hours, during which I nursed my torn hands and bruised fingers, Bulger and I were up and off again along this broad and glorious Marble Highway. Strange to say, it was not the inky darkness of the ordinary cavern which filled these magnificent chambers, through which the Marble Highway went winding in stately and massive grandeur; far from it. The gloom was tempered by a faint glow that met us on the way ever and anon, like a ray of twilight gone astray. Anyway, Bulger, I noticed, could see perfectly well; so tying a bit of twine to his collar, I sent him on ahead, convinced that I could have no surer guide.

At times our path would be lighted up for an instant by the bursting-out of a little tongue of flame either on the sides or from the roof of the gallery. I was puzzled for quite a while to tell what it proceeded from; but at last I caught sight of the source, or rather the maker, of this welcome illumination. It proceeded from a lizard-like animal, which, by suddenly uncoiling its tail, had the power to emit this extremely bright flash of phosphorescent light, and in so doing he made a sharp crack, for all the world like the noise of an electric spark. Bulger was delighted with this performance; and on one occasion, not being able to control his feeling, he uttered a sharp bark, whereupon apparently ten thousand of these little torch-bearers snapped their tails at me at the same instant, and filled the vast place with a flash of light of almost lightning-like intensity.

Bulger was so frightened by the result of his applause that he took good care to keep quiet after this.

CHAPTER VII

OUR FIRST NIGHT IN THE UNDER WORLD, AND HOW IT WAS FOLLOWED BY THE FIRST BREAK OF DAY.—BULGER'S WARNING AND WHAT IT MEANT.—WE FALL IN WITH AN INHABITANT OF THE WORLD WITHIN A WORLD.—HIS NAME AND CALLING.—MYSTERIOUS RETURN OF NIGHT.—THE LAND OF BEDS, AND HOW OUR NEW FRIEND PROVIDED ONE FOR US.

So heavy with sleep did my eyelids become at last that I knew that it must be night in the outer world, and so we halted, and I stretched myself at full length on that marble floor, which, by the way, was pleasantly warm beneath us; and the air, too, was strangely comforting to the lungs, there being a complete absence of that smell of earth and odor of dampness so common in vast subterranean chambers.

My sleep was long-continued and most refreshing; Bulger was already awake, however, when I sat up and tried to look about me.

He began tugging at the string which I had fastened to his collar as if he wanted to lead me somewhere, so I humored him and followed along after. To my delight he led me straight to a pool of deliciously sweet and cold water. Here we drank our fill, and after a very frugal breakfast on some dried figs set out again on our journey along the Marble Highway. Suddenly, to my more than joy, the faint and uncertain light of the place began to strengthen. Why, it seemed almost as if the day of the upper world were about to break, so delicate were the various hues in which the ever-increasing light clothed itself: then, as if affrighted at its own increasing glory, it would fade away again to almost gloom. Ere many moments again this faint and mysterious glow would return, beginning with the softest yellow, then changing through a dozen different tints, and, like a fickle maid uncertain which to wear, put all aside and don the lily's garb. Bulger and I wandered along the Marble Highway almost afraid to break a stillness so deep that it seemed to me as if I could hear those sportive rays of light in their play against the many-colored rocks arching this mighty corridor.

Now, as the Marble Highway swept around in a graceful curve, a dazzling flood of light burst upon us.

It was sunrise in the World within a World.

Whence came this flood of dazzling light which now caused the sides and arching roof to glow and sparkle as if we had suddenly entered one of Nature's vast storehouses of polished gems? Shading my eyes with my hand I looked about me in order to try and solve the mystery.

It did not take me long to understand it all. Know then, dear friends, that the ceilings, domes, and arched roofs of this underground world were fretted with a metal of greater hardness than any known to us children of sunshine. Its seams ran hither and thither like the veins of gigantic leaves; and at certain hours currents of electricity from some vast internal reservoir of Nature's own building, streamed through these metal traceries until they glowed with a heat so white as to give off the flood of dazzling light of which I have already spoken.

The current never came with a sudden rush or burst, but began gently and timidly, so to speak, as if feeling its way along. Hence the beautiful tints that always preceded sunrise in this lower world, and made it so much like the coming and going of our glorious sunshine.

The Marble Highway now divided, and the two halves of the fork curving away to the right and left enclosed a small but exquisitely ornamented park, or pleasure ground I might call it, provided with seats of some dark wood beautifully polished and carved. This park was ornamented with four fountains, each springing from a crystal basin and spreading out into a feathery spray that glistened like whirling snow in the dazzling white light. As Bulger and I directed our steps toward one of the benches with the intention of taking a good rest, a low growl from him warned me to be on the alert. I gave a second look. A human being was seated on the bench. Beside myself, as I was, with curiosity to come face to face with this inhabitant of the under world, the first we had met, I made a halt, determined to ascertain, if possible, whether he was quite harmless before accosting him.

He was small in stature, and clad entirely in black, a sort of loose, flowing robe much like a Roman toga. His head was bare, and what I could see of it was round, smooth, and rosy, with about as much hair, or rather fuzz, upon it as the head of an infant six weeks old. His face was hidden by a black fan which he carried in his right hand, and the uses of which you will learn later on. His eyes were shielded from the intense glare of the light by a pair of colored glass goggles. As he raised his hand between me and the light I couldn't help catching my breath. I could see right through it: the bones were as clear as amber. And his head, too, was only a little less opaque. Suddenly two words from Don Fum's manuscript flashed through my mind, and I exclaimed joyously,—

"Bulger, we're in the Land of the Transparent Folk!"

At the sound of my voice the little man arose and made a low bow, lowering his fan to his breast where he held it. His baby face was ludicrously sad and solemn.

"Yes, Sir Stranger," said he, in a low, musical voice, "thou art indeed in the Land of the Mikkamenkies (Mica Men), in the Land of the Transparent Folk, called also Goggle Land; but if I should show thee my heart thou wouldst see that I am deeply pained to think that I should have been the first to bid thee welcome, for know, Sir Stranger, that thou speakest with Master Cold Soul the Court Depressor, the saddest man in all Goggle Land, and, by the way, sir, permit me to offer thee a pair of goggles for thyself, and also a pair for thy four-footed companion, for our intense white light would blind thee both in a few days."

I thanked Master Cold Soul very warmly for the goggles, and proceeded to set one pair astride my nose and to tie the other in front of Bulger's eyes. I then in most courteous manner informed Master Cold Soul who I was, and begged him to explain the cause of his great sadness. "Well, thou must know, little baron," said he, after I had taken a seat beside him on the bench, "that we, the loving subjects of Queen Galaxa, whose royal heart is almost run down,—excuse these tears, living as we do in this beautiful world so unlike the one you inhabit, which our wise men tell us is built, strange to say, on the very outside of the earth's crust where it is most exposed to the full sweep of blinding snow, freezing blast, pelting hail, drowning rain, and choking dust,—living as we do, I say, in this vast temple by Nature's own hands builded, where disease is unknown, and where our hearts run down like clocks that may have but one winding, we are prone, alas, to be too happy; to laugh too much; to spend too much time in idle gayety, chattering the time away like thoughtless children amused with baubles, delighted with tinsel nothings. Know then, little baron, that mine is the business to check this gayety, to put an end to this childish glee, to depress our people's spirits, lest they run too high. Hence my garb of inky hue, my rueful countenance, my frequent outflowing of tears, my voice ever attuned to sadness. Excuse me, little baron, my fan slipped then; didst see through me? I would not have thee see my heart to-day, for some way or other I cannot bring it to a slow pace; it is dreadfully unruly."

I assured him that I had not seen through him as yet.

And now, dear friends, I must explain that by the laws of the Mikkamenkies each man, woman, and child must wear in their garments a heart-shaped opening on their breast directly over their hearts, with a corresponding one at the back, so that under certain conditions, when the law allows it, each may have the right to take a look at his neighbor's heart and see exactly how it is beating—whether fast or slow, whether throbbing or leaping, or whether pulsating calmly and naturally. But this privilege is only accorded, as I have said, under certain conditions, hence to shut off inquisitive glances each Mikkamenky is allowed to carry a black fan with which to cover the heart-shaped opening above described, and in this way conceal his or her feelings to a degree. I say to a degree, for I may as well tell you right here that falsehood is unknown, or, more correctly stated, impossible in the land of the Transparent Folk, for the reason that so wondrously clear, limpid, and crystal-like are their eyes that the slightest attempt to say one thing while they are thinking another roils and clouds them as if a drop of milk had fallen into a glass of the purest water.

As I sat gazing at this strange little being seated on the bench there beside me, I recalled a conversation which I had had with a learned Russian at Solvitchegodsk. Said he, speaking of his people, "We are all born with light hair, brilliant eyes, and pale faces, for we have sprung up under the snow." And I thought to myself how delighted, how entranced, he would have been to look upon this curious being, born not under the snow, but far under the surface of the earth, where in these vast chambers of this World within a World, this strange folk had, like plants grown in a dark, deep cellar, gradually parted with all their coloring until their eyes glowed like orbs of pure crystal, until their bones had been bleached to amber clearness, and their blood coursed colorless through colorless veins. While sitting there following out this train of thought, the clear white light suddenly began to flicker and to play fantastic tricks upon the walls by dancing in garbs of ever-changing hues, now brightest yellow, now palest green, now glorious purple, now deepest crimson.

"Ah, little baron!" exclaimed Master Cold Soul, "that was an uncommonly short day. Rise, please."

I made haste to obey, whereupon he touched a spring and the bench opened in the centre, disclosing two very comfortable beds.

A DINNER EASILY PROVIDED FOR.

"In a few moments night will be upon us," continued the Mikkamenky, "but thou seest that we have not been taken by surprise. I should explain to thee, little baron, that owing to the capricious manner in which our River of Light is apt both to begin and to cease flowing, we are never able to tell how long a day or a night will prove to be. This is what we call twilight. In thy world I suppose day goes out with a terrible bang, for our wise men tell us that nothing can be done in the upper world without making a noise; that your people really love noise; and that the man who makes the greatest noise is considered the greatest man.

"Owing to the fact, little baron, that no one in Goggle Land can tell how long the day will last, or how long it may be necessary to sleep, our laws permit no one to set any exact time when a thing shall be done, or to exact any promise to do this or that on a certain day, for, bless thy soul, that day may not be ten minutes long. Hence we say, 'If to-morrow be over five hours long, come to me at the beginning of the sixth hour;' and we never wish each other a plain good-night, but say, 'Good-night, as long as it lasts.'

"What's more, little baron, as night is apt to come upon us this way unawares, by law all the beds belong to the state; no one is allowed to own his own bed, for when night overtakes him he may be at the other end of the city, and some other subject of Queen Galaxa may be in front of his door, and no matter where night may overtake a Mikkamenky, he is sure to find a bed. There are beds everywhere. By touching a spring they drop from the walls, they pull out like drawers, they are under the tables and divans, in the parks, in the market-place, by the roadside; benches, bins, boxes, barrows, and barrels by pressing a spring may in an instant be transformed into beds. It is the Land of Beds, little baron. But ah! behold, the twilight goes to its end. Good-night as long as it lasts!" and with this Master Cold Soul stretched himself out and began to snore, having first carefully covered up the two holes in the front and back of his garment, so that I shouldn't have a chance to take a peep through him in case I should wake up first. Bulger and I were right glad to lay our limbs on a real bed, although from the way my four-footed brother followed his tail around and around, I could see that he wasn't particularly delighted with the softness of the couch.

CHAPTER VIII

"GOOD-MORNING AS LONG AS IT LASTS."—PLAIN TALK FROM MASTER COLD SOUL.—WONDERS OF GOGGLE LAND.—WE ENTER THE CITY OF THE MIKKAMENKIES.—BRIEF DESCRIPTION OF IT.—OUR APPROACH TO THE ROYAL PALACE.—QUEEN GALAXA AND HER CRYSTAL THRONE.—MASTER COLD SOUL'S TEARS.

I don't think the darkness lasted over three hours, perhaps it was longer; but Master Cold Soul was obliged to shake me gently ere he could rouse me.

"Now, little baron," said he, after he had wished me a good-morning with the usual "as long as it lasts" tacked to it, "if thou art quite willing, I'll conduct thee to the court of our gracious mistress, Queen Galaxa. Our wise men have often discoursed to her concerning the upper world and the terrible sufferings of its people, exposed as they are to be first frozen by the pitiless cold and then burned by the scorching rays of what they call their sun, and she will no doubt deign to be pleased at sight of thee, although I must warn thee that thou art most uncomely, that thou seemst so black and hard to me as scarcely to be human, but rather a bit of living earth or rock. I greatly fear me that thou wilt make our people extremely vain by comparison. Thy four-footed companion we know well by sight, having often seen his petrified image in the rocks of the dark chambers of our world."

"Master Cold Soul," said I, as we walked along, "when thou gettest to know me better thou wilt find me more comely, and although I shall not be able to show thee my heart, I hope to be able to prove to thee and thine that I have such a thing."

"No doubt, no doubt, little baron," exclaimed Master Cold Soul, "but be not offended. It is not more pleasant for me to tell thee these disagreeable things than it is for thee to hear them, but I am paid to do it and I must earn my wage. Vanity grows apace in our world, and I prick its bubbles whenever I see them."

To my great wonder I now discovered that the world of the Mikkamenkies had its lakes and rivers like our own, only of course they were smaller and mirror-faced, being never visited by the faintest zephyr. To my question as to whether they were peopled with living things, Master Cold Soul informed me that they literally swarmed with the most delicious fish, both in scales and shells.

"But think not, little baron," he added, "that we of Goggle Land have no other food than such as we draw from the water; for in our gardens grow many kinds of delicate vegetables, springing up in a single night almost as light as foam and just as white. But we are small eaters, little baron, and rarely find it necessary to put to death a large shellfish. We merely lay hold of his great claw, which he obligingly drops into our hand, and forthwith sets about growing another."

"But tell me, I pray thee, Master Cold Soul," said I, "where ye find the silk to weave such soft and beautiful stuff as that thy garment is fashioned from?"

"In this under world of ours, little baron," replied Master Cold Soul, "there are many vast recesses not reached by the River of Light, and in these dark chambers flit about huge night moths, like restless spirits forever on the wing, but of course they are not, for we find their eggs glued against the rocky sides of these caverns and collect them carefully. The worms that are hatched from them spin huge cocoons so large that one may not be hidden in my hand, and these unwound give unto our looms all the thread they need."

"And the beautiful wood," I continued, "which I see about me carved and fashioned into so many articles, whence comes it?"

"From the quarries," answered Master Cold Soul.

"Quarries?" I repeated wonderingly.

"Why, yes, little baron," said he, "for we have quarries of wood as no doubt thou hast quarries of stone. Our wise men tell us that thousands and thousands of years ago vast forests grown in your world were in the upheavals and fallings-in of the earth's crust thrust down into ours, the gigantic trunks wedged closely together, and standing bolt upright just as they grew. At least, so we find them when we have dug away the hardened clay that has shut them in these many ages. But see, little baron, we are now entering the city. Yonder is the royal palace—wilt walk with me thither?"

Ah, dear friends, would that I could make you see this beautiful city of the under world just as it showed itself to me then, spread out so gloriously beneath the glittering domes and vaulted corridors, from which poured down upon the exquisitely carved and polished entrances to the living chambers of this happy folk, a flood of white light apparently more dazzling than our noonday sun!

It was a sight so strangely beautiful that many times I paused to gaze upon it. Young and old, all clad in the same gracefully flowing garbs of silk, now purple, now royal blue, and now rich vermilion, were hurrying hither and thither, each armed with the inevitable black fan, and the baby face of each aglow with life and sweet content, while a hundred fountains springing from crystal basins glistened in the dazzling white light, and ten times a hundred flags and gonfalons hung listless but rich in splendor from invisible wires. Strange music came floating along from the gracefully shaped barges with silken awnings, which were gliding noiselessly over the surface of the winding river, the oars stirring the waters until the wake seemed a path through molten silver.

As Bulger and I followed Master Cold Soul along the streets of polished marble, it was not long before a crowd of Mikkamenkies was at our heels, whispering all sorts of uncomplimentary things about us, mingled with not a few fits of suppressed laughter.

The Court Depressor reproved them sternly.

"Cease your ill-timed mirth," said he, "and go about your business. Must I pause and tell you a grewsome tale to check your foolish gayety? Know ye not that all this silly mirth doth quicken your hearts and make them run down just so much sooner?"

At these words of Master Cold Soul they fell back, and put an end to their giggling, but it was only for a moment, and by the time we reached the portal of the royal palace, a still louder and noisier crowd was close behind us.

Master Cold Soul suddenly halted, and drawing forth a huge pocket-handkerchief, began to weep furiously. It was not without its effect, and from that moment I could see that the Mikkamenkies were inclined to take a more serious view of my arrival in their city, although it was only Cold Soul's presence that kept them from bursting out into fits of violent laughter.

Above the portals of the queen's palace there were large openings hewn in the rock for the purpose of admitting light into the royal apartments; but these windows, if they may be called such, were hung with silken curtains of delicate colors, so that the light which entered the throne room was tempered and softened. The room itself was likewise hung with silken stuffs, which gave it a look of Oriental splendor; but never in my travels among strange peoples of far-away lands had my eyes ever rested upon any work of art that equalled the crystal throne upon which sat Galaxa, Queen of the Mikkamenkies.

In the upper world most diligent search had never been able to unearth a piece of rock crystal more than about three feet in diameter; but here in Queen Galaxa's throne four glorious columns at least fifteen feet in height, and at their base three feet in diameter, shot up in matchless splendor. Their lower parts shut in spangles of gold that glittered with ever-varying hues as a different light fell upon them. The cross pieces and pieces making up the back and arms had been chosen on account of the exquisitely beautiful hair and needle-shaped crystals of other metals which they enclosed. A silken baldachin of rare beauty covered in the throne, and from its edges dropped heavy cords and tassels of rich color and the perfection of human handicraft as to fineness and finish.

At the foot of the throne sat the young princess Crystallina; and standing behind her, and engaged in combing her long silken tresses, was her favorite waiting-maid, Damozel Glow Stone, while around and about, in files and groupwise, stood lords and ladies, courtiers and counsellors, by the dozen.

As Master Cold Soul advanced to salute the queen, a throng of the idlers who had followed at our heels crowded into the anteroom with loud outbursts of laughter. The Court Depressor was greatly incensed, and turning upon the throng he began weeping again with wonderful energy; but I noticed that it was nothing but sound: not a tear fell to obscure the crystal clearness of his eyes. Then he began chanting a sort of song which was intended to have a depressing influence on the wild mirth of the Mikkamenkies. I can only recollect one verse of this solemn chant of the Court Depressor. It ran as follows:—

"Weep, Mikkamenkies, weep, O weep,
  For the eyeless man in the City of Light,
  For the mouthless man in Plenty's bowers,
  For the earless man in Music's realm,
  For the noseless man in the Kingdom of flowers,
Weep, Mikkamenkies, weep, O weep!"

But they only laughed the louder, crying out,—

"Nay, Master Cold Soul, we will not weep for them; weep for them thyself." At last Queen Galaxa raised the slender golden wand, tipped with a diamond point, that lay within her hand, and instantly a hush came upon the whole place, while every eye was riveted upon Bulger and me.

CHAPTER IX

BULGER AND I ARE PRESENTED TO QUEEN GALAXA, THE LADY OF THE CRYSTAL THRONE.—HOW SHE RECEIVED US.—HER DELIGHT OVER BULGER, WHO GIVES PROOF OF HIS WONDERFUL INTELLIGENCE IN MANY WAYS.—HOW THE QUEEN CREATES HIM LORD BULGER.—ALL ABOUT THE THREE WISE MEN IN WHOSE CARE WE ARE PLACED BY QUEEN GALAXA.

Owing to the soft air, the never-varying temperature, and the absence of all noise and dust, the Mikkamenkies, although they die in the end like other folk, yet do they never seem to grow old. Their skin remains soft and free from wrinkles, and their eyes as clear and bright as the crystal of Queen Galaxa's throne.

At the time of our arrival in the Land of the Transparent Folk, Queen Galaxa's heart had almost run down. In about two weeks more it would come quietly and gently to a stop; for, as I have already told you, dear friends, the heart of a Mikkamenky being perfectly visible when the dazzling white light in its full strength was allowed to shine through his body, why, it was a very easy matter for a physician to take a look at the organ of life, and tell almost to the hour when it would exhaust itself—in other words, run down. Galaxa looked every inch a real queen as she half-reclined upon her glorious crystal throne. She was clad in long, flowing silk garments of a right royal purple, and the gems which encircled her neck and wrists would have put to shame the crown jewels of any monarch of the upper world. Her garb had very much the cut and style of the ancient Greek costume, and the gold sandals worn by her added to the resemblance; but the one thing that excited my wonder more than all the others put together was her hair, so long, so fine and silken was it, such a mass of it was there, and so dazzling white was it—not the blue or yellow white that comes of age in our world, but a milk white, a cotton white. And as we drew near, to Bulger's but not to my amazement, her hair began to quiver and rustle and rise, until it buried her whole throne completely out of sight. Of course I knew that, seated as she was upon a throne of glass, it was only necessary to send a gentle current of electricity through her to make her wonderful head of hair stand up in this manner, like the white and filmy tentacles of some gigantic creature of the sea, half-plant, half-animal.

"Rise, little baron," said Queen Galaxa, as I dropped upon my right knee on the lowest step of the throne, "and be welcome to our kingdom. Whilst thou may be pleased to tarry here, my people shall bestir themselves to show thee all that may seem wonderful in thine eyes; for although our wise men have often discussed to us of the upper world, yet art thou its first inhabitant to visit us, and thy wonderful companion is right welcome too. Can he talk, little baron?"

"Not exactly, Queen Galaxa," said I with low obeisance, "yet he can understand me and I him."

"He is quite harmless, is he not?" asked the queen.

You may try to imagine how I felt, dear friends, when as I was about to say, "Perfectly so, royal lady," to my amazement I saw Bulger advance and sniff at the Princess

Crystallina and then draw back and show his teeth as she stretched out her hand to caress him.

Bending over him I reproved him in a whisper, and bade him kneel before the queen. This he proceeded to do, saluting her with three very stately bows, at which everybody laughed heartily.

"I would have him come nearer," said the queen, "so that I may lay my hand upon him."

At a sign from me Bulger began to lick his fore-paws very carefully, and then having wiped them on the rug, sprang up the steps of the throne and placed his front feet upon Queen Galaxa's lap.

The fair ruler of the Mikkamenkies was delighted with this sample of Bulger's fine manners, and in order to amuse her still further I proceeded to put Bulger through many of his quaint tricks and curious feats, bidding him "say his prayers," "feign death," "weep for his sweetheart," "count ten," "walk upright," "go lame and cry to tell how it hurts."

Scarcely had he gone half around the circle, feigning lameness, when the damozel Glow Stone began to weep herself, and stooping down commenced to caress Bulger and to kiss his lame foot, caresses which, to my more than surprise, Bulger was not slow in returning, and later too when I bade him choose the maiden he loved best and kiss her hand, he bounded straight toward Glow Stone and bestowed not one but twenty kisses upon her outstretched hands, while the princess Crystallina shrank away in fear and disgust from the "ugly beast," as she termed him.

"Bid him bring my handkerchief to me, little baron," cried Galaxa, throwing it on the floor. I did as the queen commanded, but Bulger refused to obey.

"Thou seest, Queen Galaxa," said I with a low bow, "he refuses to lift the handkerchief without a command from thy royal self," which delicate compliment pleased the lady mightily.

"How comes it, little baron," she asked, "that thou shouldst be of noble lineage and thy brother, as thou callest him, plain Bulger?"

"It comes, royal lady," said I right humbly, "as it often comes in the world which I inhabit, that honors go to them that least deserve them."

"Well, then, little baron," cried Galaxa gayly, "though I be but a petty sovereign compared with thine, yet may small rulers do acts of great justice. Bid thy four-footed brother kneel before us."

PRINCESS CRYSTALLINA UNCOVERS HER HEART.

At a word from me, Bulger prostrated himself on the steps of Galaxa's crystal throne, and laid his head at her very feet.

Leaning forward she touched him lightly with her golden wand, and exclaimed, "Rise, Lord Bulger, rise! Queen Galaxa seated on her crystal throne bids Lord Bulger rise!"

In an instant Bulger raised himself on his hind feet and laid his head in the queen's lap, while the whole room rang with loud huzzas, and every lady gently clapped her frail and glass-like hands, save the princess Crystallina who feigned to be asleep.

Queen Galaxa now undid a string of pearls from her neck and tied them with her own hands around Lord Bulger's—and so it was that my four-footed brother ceased to be plain Bulger. Then turning to her counsellors of state, Queen Galaxa bade them assign a royal apartment to Lord Bulger and me, and gave strict orders that the severest punishment be at once visited upon any Mikkamenky who should dare to laugh at us or to make disrespectful remarks concerning our dark eyes and skins and weather-beaten appearance, for, as the royal lady said to her people, "Ye might look worse than they were ye compelled to live on the outside instead of the inside of the world, exposed to biting blasts, piercing cold, and clouds of suffocating dust."

By the queen's orders three of the wisest of the Mikkamenkies were selected to attend Bulger and me, look after our wants, explain everything to us—in a word, do all in their power to make our stay in Goggle Land as pleasant as possible.

Their names, as nearly as I can translate them, were Doctor Nebulosus, Sir Amber O'Pake, and Lord Cornucore. I should explain to you, dear friends, the meaning of these names, for you might be inclined to think that Doctor Somewhat Cloudy, Sir Clear-as-Amber; and Lord Heart-of-Horn might indicate that they were more or less muddled in their intellects. Far from it: I have already stated to you they were three of the very wisest men in the Land of the Transparent Folk, and the lack of clearness indicated by their names had reference solely to their eyes.

Now, as you know, the learned men of our upper world have a different look from ordinary folk. They are stoop-shouldered, shaggy-eyebrowed, long-haired, pursed-lipped, near-sighted, shambling-gaited. Well, the only effect that long years of deep study had upon the Mikkamenkies was to rob their beautiful crystal-like eyes of more or less of their clearness.

Now I think you'll understand why these three learned Mikkamenkies were named as they were.

At any rate, they were, in spite of their strange names, three most charming gentlemen; and no matter how many times I might ask the same question over again, they were always ready with an answer quite as polite as the one first given me. They did everything that I had a right possibly to expect them to do. Indeed, there was but one single thing which I would have fain had them do, and that was to let me look through them.

This they most carefully avoided doing; and no matter how warmed up they might become in their descriptions, and no matter how on the alert I was to catch the coveted peep, the inevitable black fan was always in the way.

Naturally, not only they, but all the Transparent Folk, felt a repugnance to have a perfect stranger look through them, and I couldn't blame them for it either. I despaired of ever getting a chance of seeing a human heart beating away for dear life, for all the world just like the swing of a pendulum or the vibration of a balance wheel.

CHAPTER X

A BRIEF ACCOUNT OF MY CONVERSATIONS WITH DOCTOR NEBULOSUS, SIR AMBER O'PAKE, AND LORD CORNUCORE, WHO TELL ME MANY THINGS THAT I NEVER KNEW BEFORE, FOR WHICH I WAS VERY GRATEFUL.

Lord Bulger and I were more than pleased with our new friends, Doctor Nebulosus, Sir Amber O'Pake, and Lord Cornucore, although so eager were they to make us thoroughly comfortable, that they overdid the matter at times, and left me scarcely a moment to myself in which to make an entry in my notebook. They were extremely solicitous lest in my ignorance I should set down something wrong about them.

"For," said Sir Amber O'Pake, "now that thou hast found the way to this under world of ours, little baron, I feel assured that we shall have a number of visitors from thy people every year or so, and I have already issued orders to have extra beds made as soon as the wood can be quarried."

Doctor Nebulosus gave me a very interesting account of the various ailments which the Mikkamenkies suffer from. "All sickness among our people, little baron," said he, "is purely mental or emotional; that is, of the mind or feelings. There is no such thing as bodily infirmity among us. Wine and strong drink are unknown in our world, and the food we eat is light and easily digested. We are never exposed to the danger of breathing a dust-laden atmosphere, and while we are an active and industrious people, yet we sleep a great deal; for, as our laws forbid the use of lamps or torches, except for the use of those toiling in the dark chambers, it is not possible for us to ruin our health by turning night into day. We go to bed the very moment the River of Light ceases to flow. The only ailment that ever gives me the least trouble is *iburyufrosnia*."

"Pray, what is the nature of that ailment?" I asked.

"It is an inclination to be too happy," replied Doctor Nebulosus gravely, "and I regret to say that several of our people attacked with this ailment have shortened their lives by refusing to take my remedies. It usually develops very slowly, beginning with an inclination to giggle, which, after a while, is succeeded by violent fits of laughter.

"For instance, little baron, when thou camest among us, many of our people were attacked with a violent form of *iburyufrosnia*; and although Master Cold Soul, the Court Depressor, made great efforts to check it, yet he was quite powerless to do so. It spread over the city with remarkable rapidity. Without knowing why, our workmen at their work, our children at their play, our people in doors and out, began to laugh and to be dangerously happy. I made examinations of several of the worst cases, and discovered that at the rate they were beating the hearts of most of them would run down in a single week. It was terrible. A council was hastily held, and it was determined to conceal thee and Lord Bulger from the public view, but happily my skill got the upper hand of the attack."

"Didst increase the number of pills to be taken?" I asked.

"No, little baron," said Doctor Nebulosus; "I increased their size and covered them with a dry powder, which made them extremely difficult to swallow, and in this way compelled those taking them to cease their laughing. But there were a number of cases so violent that they could not be cured in this way. These I ordered to be strapped in at the waist with broad belts, and to have their mouths held pried open with wooden wedges. As thou mayst understand, this made laughing so difficult that they speedily gave it up altogether.

"Ah, little baron," continued the wise doctor with a sigh, "that was a sorry day for the human race when it learned how to laugh. It is my opinion that we owe this useless agitation of our bodies to you people of the upper world. Exposed as ye were to piercing winds and biting frosts, ye contracted the habit of shivering to keep warm, and, little by little, this shivering habit so grew upon you, that ye kept up the shivering whether ye were cold or not; only ye called it by another name. Now, my knowledge of the human body teaches me that this quivering of the flesh is a very wise provision of nature to keep the blood in motion, and in this way to save the human body from perishing from the cold; but why should we quiver when we are happy, little baron? All pleasure is the thought, and yet at the very moment when we should keep our bodies in as perfect repose as possible, we begin this ridiculous shivering. Do we shiver when we look upon the beauties of the River of Light, or listen to sweet music, or gaze upon the loving countenance of our gracious Queen Galaxa? But worse than all, little baron, this senseless quivering and shivering which we call laughter, unlike good, deep, long-drawn, wholesome sighs, empty the lungs of air without filling them again, and thus do we often see these gigglers and laughers fall over in fainting fits, absolutely choked by their own wild and unreasoning action. I have always contended, little baron, that we alone of all animals had the laughing habit, and I am now delighted to have my opinion confirmed by my acquaintance with the wise and dignified Lord Bulger. Observe him. He knows quite as well as we what it is to be pleased, to be amused, to be delighted, but he doesn't think it necessary to have recourse to fits of shivering and shuddering. Through the brightened eye—true window of the soul—I can see how happy he is. I can measure his joy; I can take note of his contentment."

I was delighted with this learned discourse of the gentle Doctor Nebulosus, and made notes of it lest the points of his argument might escape my memory, the more pleased was I in that he proved my faithful Bulger to be so wisely constructed and regulated by nature.

I made particular inquiry of my friends, Sir Amber O'Pake and Lord Cornucore, as to whether Queen Galaxa ever had any trouble in governing her people.

"None whatever," was the answer. "In many a long year has it only been necessary on one or two occasions to summon a Mikkamenky before the magistrate and examine his heart under a strong light. The only punishment allowed by our laws is confinement for a shorter or longer time in one of the dark chambers. The severest sentence ever known to have been passed by one of our magistrates was twelve hours in length. But in all honesty, we must admit, little baron, that falsehood and deception are unknown amongst us for the simple reason that, being transparent, it is impossible for a Mikkamenky to deceive a brother without being caught in the act. Therefore why make the attempt? The very moment one of us begins to say one thing while he is thinking another, his eyes cloud up and betray him, just as the crystal-clear weather glass clouds up at the approach of a storm in the upper world. But this, of course, little baron, is only true of our thoughts. Our laws allow us to hide our feelings by the use of the black fan. No one may look upon another's heart unless its owner wills it. It is a very grave offence for one Mikkamenky to look through another without that one's permission. But as thou wilt readily understand, inasmuch as we are by nature transparent, it is utterly impossible for a marriage to prove an unhappy one, for the reason that when a youth declares his love for a maiden, they both have the right by law to look upon each other's hearts, and in this way they can tell exactly the strength of the love they have for each other." This and many other strange and interesting things did my new friends, Doctor Nebulosus, Sir Amber O'Pake, and Lord Cornucore impart unto me, and right grateful was I to good Queen Galaxa for having chosen them for me. Good friends are better than gold, although we may not think it at the time.

CHAPTER XI

PLEASANT DAYS PASSED AMONG THE MIKKAMENKIES, AND WONDERFUL THINGS SEEN BY US.—THE SPECTRAL GARDEN, AND A DESCRIPTION OF IT.—OUR MEETING WITH DAMOZEL GLOW STONE, AND WHAT CAME OF IT.

From now on Lord Bulger and I made ourselves perfectly at home among the Mikkamenkies. One of the royal barges was placed at our disposal, and when we grew tired of walking about and gazing at the wonders of this beautiful city of the under world, we stepped aboard our barge and were rowed hither and thither on the glassy river; and if I had not seen it myself I never would have believed that any kind of shellfish could ever be taught to be so obliging as to swim to the surface and offer one of their huge claws for our dinner, politely dropping it in our hand the moment we had laid hold of it. On one of the river banks I noticed a long row of wooden compartments looking very much like a grocer's bins; but you may think how amused Bulger and I were upon coming closer to this long row of little houses to find that they were turtle nests, and that quite a number of the turtles were sitting comfortably in their nests busy laying their eggs—which, let me assure you, were the most dainty tidbits I ever tasted.

I think I informed you that the river flowing through Goggle Land was fairly swarming with delicious fish, the carp and sole being particularly delicate in flavor; and knowing, as I did, what a tender-hearted folk the

Mikkamenkies are, I had been not a little puzzled in my mind as to how they had ever been able to summon up courage enough to drive a spear into one of these fish, which were as tame and playful as a lot of kittens or puppies, and followed our barge hither and thither, snapping up the food we tossed to them, and leaping into the air, where they glistened like burnished silver as the white light sparkled on their scales.

But the mystery was solved one day when I saw one of the fishermen decoying a score or more of fish into a sort of pen shut off from the river by a wire netting. Scarcely had he closed the gates when, to my amazement, I saw the fish one after the other come to the surface and float about on their sides, stone dead.

"This, little baron," explained the man in charge, "is the death chamber. Hidden at the bottom of this dark pool lie several electric eels of great size and power, and when our people want a fresh supper of fish we simply open these gates and decoy a shoal of them inside by tossing their favorite food into the water. The executioners are awaiting them, and in a few instants the fish, while enjoying their repast and suspecting no harm, are painlessly put to death, as thou hast seen."

One part of the city of the Transparent Folk which attracted Bulger and me very much was the royal gardens. It was a weird and uncanny place, and upon my first visit I walked through its paths and beneath its arbors upon my toes and with bated breath, as you might steal into some bit of fairy-land, looking anxiously from side to side as if at every step you expected some sprite or goblin to trip you up with a tough spider-web, or brush your cheeks with their cold and satiny wings.

Now, dear friends, you must first be told that with the loss of sunshine and the open air, the flowers and shrubs and vines of this underground world gradually parted with their perfumes and colors, their leaves and petals and stems and tendrils growing paler and paler in hue, like lovelorn maids whose sweethearts had never come back from the war. Month by month the dark greens, the blush pinks, the golden yellows, and the deep blues pined away, longing for the lost sunshine and the wooing breeze they loved so dearly, until at last the transformation was complete, and there they all stood or hung bleached to utter whiteness, like those fantastic clumps of flowers and wreaths of vines which the feathery snow of April builds in the leafless shrubs and trees.

I cannot tell you, dear friends, what a strange feeling came over me as I stepped within this spectral garden where ghost-like vines clung in fantastic forms and figures to the dark trellises, and where tall lilies, whiter than the down of eider, stood bolt upright like spirits doomed to eternal silence, denied even the speech of perfume, and where huge clusters of snowy chrysanthemums, fluffy feathery forms, seemed pressing their soft bodies together like groups of banished celestials in a sort of silent despair as they felt the warmth and glow of sunlight slowly and gradually quitting their souls; where lower down, great roses with snowy petals whiter than the sea-shells hung motionless, bursting open with eager effort, as if listening for some signal that would dissolve the spell put upon them, and give them back the sunshine, and with it their color and their perfume; where lower still beds of violets bleached white as fleecy clouds seemed wrapt in silent sorrow at loss of the heavenly perfume which had been theirs on earth; where, above the lilies' heads shot long, slender, spectral stalks of sunflowers almost invisible, loaded at their ends with clusters of snowy flowers thus suspended like white faces looking down through the silent air, and waiting, waiting for the sunshine that never came; and higher still all over and above these spectral flowers, intwining and inwrapping and falling festoon and garlandwise, crept and ran like unto long lines of escaping phantoms, ghostly vines with ghostly blossoms, bent and twisted and wrapped and coiled into a thousand strange and fantastic forms and figures which the white light with its inky shadows made alive and half human, so that movement and voice alone were needful to make this garden seem peopled with sorrowing sprites banished to these subterranean chambers for strange misdeeds done on earth and condemned to wait ten thousand years ere sunlight and their color and their perfume should be given back to them again.

While strolling through the royal gardens one day, Bulger suddenly gave a low cry and bounded on ahead, as if his eyes had fallen upon the familiar form of some dear friend.

When I came up with him he was crouching beside the damozel Glow Stone who, seated on one of the garden benches, was caressing Bulger's head and ears with one of her soft hands with its filmy-like skin, while the other held its black fan pressed tightly against her bosom.

She looked up at me with her crystal eyes, and smiled faintly as I drew near.

"Thou seest, little baron," she murmured, "Lord Bulger and I have not forgotten each other." Since our presentation at court I had been going through and through my mind in search of some reason for Bulger's sudden affection for damozel Glow Stone, but had found none.

I was the more perplexed as she was but the maid of honor, while the fair princess Crystallina sat on the very steps of the throne.

But I said nothing save to reply that I was greatly pleased to see it and to add that where Bulger's love went, mine was sure to follow.

"Oh, little baron, if I could but believe that!" sighed the fair damozel.

"Thou mayst," said I, "indeed thou mayst."

"Then, if I may, little baron," she replied, "I will, and prithee come and sit beside me here, only till I bid thee, look not through me. Dost promise?"

"I do, fair damozel," was my answer.

"And thou, Lord Bulger, lie there at my feet," she continued, "and keep thy wise eyes fixed upon me and thy keen ears wide open."

"Little baron, if both thine and our worlds were filled with sorrowing hearts, mine would be the heaviest of them all. List! oh, list to the sad, sad tale of the sorrowing maid with the speck in her heart, and, when thou knowest all, give me of thy wisdom."

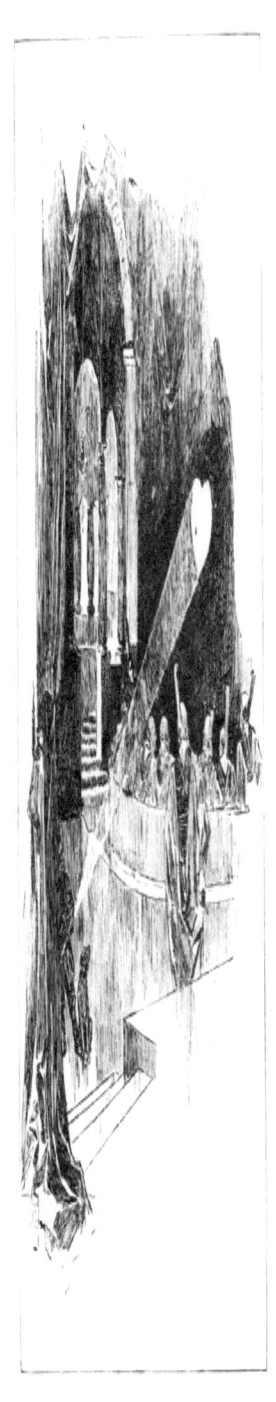

CRYSTALLINA'S HEART ON A SCREEN.

CHAPTER XII

THE SAD, SAD TALE OF THE SORROWING PRINCESS WITH A SPECK IN HER HEART, AND WHAT ALL HAPPENED WHEN SHE HAD ENDED IT, WHICH THE READER MUST READ FOR HIMSELF IF HE WOULD KNOW.

"Little baron and dear Lord Bulger," began the crystal-eyed damozel, after she had eased her soul of its load of woe by three long and deep, deep sighs, "know then that I am not the damozel Glow Stone, but none other than the royal princess Crystallina herself; that she whose hair I comb should comb mine; that she whom I have served for ten long years should have served me!"

"And to think, O princess," I burst out joyfully, "that my beloved Bulger should have been the first to discover that she who was seated on the steps of the crystal throne was not entitled to the seat; to think that his subtle intellect should have been the first to scent out the wrong that had been done thee; his keen eye the first to go to the bottom of truth's well; but, fair princess, I am bursting with impatience to know how thou thyself didst ever discover the wrong that has been done thee."

"That thou shalt speedily know, little baron," answered Crystallina, "and that thou mayst know all that I know I'll begin at the very beginning: The day I was born there was great rejoicing in the land of the Mikkamenkies, and the people gathered in front of the royal palace and laughed and cried by turns, so happy were they to think they were to be governed by another princess after Queen Galaxa's heart should run down; for, many years ago, a bad king had made them very unhappy, and they had hoped and prayed that no more such would come to reign over them. And pretty soon one of them began to tell the others what he thought the little princess would be like.

"'She will be the fairest that ever sat upon the crystal throne. Her hands and feet will be like pearls tipped with coral; her hair whiter than the river's foam; and from her beautiful eyes will burst the radiance of her pure soul, and her heart, Oh, her heart will be like a little lump of frozen water so clear and so transparent will it be, so like a bit of purest crystal, bright and flawless as a diamond of the first water, and therefore let her be called the princess Crystallina, or the Maid with the Crystal Heart.'

"Forthwith the cry went up: 'Ay, let her be called Crystallina, or the Maid with the Crystal Heart,' and Queen Galaxa heard the cry of her people and sent them word that it should be as they wished—that I should be the Princess Crystallina.

"But, ah me, that I should have lived to tell it! after a few days the nurse came to my royal mother wringing her hands and pouring down a flood of tears.

"Throwing herself on her knees, she whispered to the queen, 'Royal mistress, bid me die rather than tell thee what I know.'

"Being ordered to speak, the nurse informed Queen Galaxa that she had that day for the first time held me up to the light and had discovered that there was a speck in my heart.

"The queen uttered a cry of horror and swooned. When she came to herself she directed that I should be brought to her and held up to the light so that she might see for herself. Alas, too true! there was the speck in my heart sure enough. I was not worthy of the sweet name which her loving people had bestowed upon me. They would turn from me with horror; they would never consent to have me for their queen when the truth should become known. They would not be moved by a mother's prayers: they would turn a deaf ear to every one who should be bold enough to advise them to accept a princess with a speck in her heart, when they had thought they were getting one well deserving of the title they had bestowed upon her.

"Queen Galaxa knew that something must be done at once; that it would be time and labor lost to attempt to reason with the disappointed people, so she set to work thinking up some way out of her trouble. Now, it so happened, little baron, that the very day I had come into the world a babe had been born to one of Queen Galaxa's serving women; and so hastily summoning the woman she ordered her to bring her babe into the royal bed-chamber and leave it there, promising that it should be brought up as my foster-sister. But no sooner had the serving woman gone her way rejoicing than the nurse was ordered to change the children in the cradle, and in a few moments Glow Stone was wrapt in my richly embroidered blanket and I swathed up in her plain coverlets.

"How things went for several years I know not, but one day, ah, how well I recollect it! my little mind was puzzled by hearing Crystallina cry out: 'Nay, nay, dear mamma, 'tis not fair; I like it not. Each day when thou comest to us thou givest Glow Stone ten kisses and me but a single one.' Then would Queen Galaxa smile a sad smile and bestow some bauble upon Crystallina to coax her back to contentment again.

"And so we went on, Crystallina and I, from one year to another until we were little maids well grown, and she sat on the throne and wore royal purple stitched with gold, and I plain white; but still most of the kisses fell to my share.

And I marvelled not a little at it, but dared not ask why it was. However, once when I was alone with Queen Galaxa, seated on my cushion in the corner plying my needle and thinking of the sail we were to have on the river that day, suddenly I was startled to see the queen throw herself on her knees in front of me, and to feel her clasp me in her arms and cover my face and head with tears and kisses, as she sobbed and moaned,—

"'O my babe, my lost babe, my blessing and my joy, wilt never, never, never come back to me? Art gone forever? Must I give thee up, oh, must I?'"

"'Nay, Royal Lady,' I stammered in my more than wonder at her words and actions. 'Thou art in a dream. Awake, and see clearly; I am not Crystallina. I am Glow Stone, thy foster-child. I'll hie me straight and bring my royal sister to thee.'

"But she would not let me loose, and for all answer showered more kisses on me till I was well-nigh smothered, so tight she held me pressed against her bosom, while around and over me her long thick tresses fell like a woven mantle.

"And then she told me all—all that I have told thee, little baron, and charged me never to impart it unto any soul in Goggle Land; and I made a solemn promise unto her that I never would."

"And thou hast kept thy word like a true princess as thou art," said I cheerily, "for I am not of thy world, fair Crystallina."

"Now that I have told thee the sad tale of the sorrowing princess with the speck in her heart, little baron," murmured Crystallina, fixing her large and radiant eyes upon me, "there is but one thing more for me to do, and it is to let thee look through me, so that thou mayst know exactly what counsel to give." And so saying the fair princess rose from her seat, and having placed herself in front of me with a flood of white light falling full upon her back, she lowered her black fan and bade me gaze upon the heavy heart which she had carried about with her all these years, and tell her exactly how large the speck was and where it lay, and what color it was.

I was overjoyed to get an opportunity at last to look through one of the Mikkamenkies, and my own heart bounded with satisfaction as I looked and looked upon that mysterious little thing, nay, rather a tiny being, living, breathing, palpitating within her breast; now slow and measured as she dwelt in thought upon her sad fate, now beating faster and faster as the hope bubbled up in her mind that possibly I might be able to counsel her so wisely that an end would come to all her sorrow.

"Well, wise little baron," she murmured anxiously, "what seest thou? Is it very large? In what part is it? Is it black as night or some color less fatal?"

"Take courage, fair princess," said I, "it is very small and lies just beneath the bow on the left side. Nor is it black, but reddish rather, as if a single drop of blood from the veins of thy far distant ancestors had outlived them these thousands of years and hardened there to tell whence thy people came." The princess wept tears of joy upon hearing these comforting words.

"If it had been black," she whispered "I would have lain me down in this bed of violets and never risen more till my people had come to bear me to my grave in the silent burial chamber—unvisited by the River of Light."

At this sad outbreak Bulger whined piteously and licked the princess's hands as he looked up at her with his dark eyes radiant with sympathy.

She was greatly cheered by this message of comfort, and it moved me, too, by its heartiness.

"List, fair princess," said I gravely. "I own the task is not a light one, but hope for the best. I would that we had more time, but as thou knowest Queen Galaxa's heart will soon run down, therefore must we act with despatch as well as wisdom. But first of all must I speak with the queen and gain her consent to act for thee in this matter."

"That, I fear me, she will never grant," moaned Crystallina. "However, thou art so much wiser than I—do as best seems to thee."

"The next thing to be done, fair princess," I added solemnly, "is to show thy heart boldly and fearlessly to thy people."

"Nay, little baron," she exclaimed, rising to her feet, "that may not be, that may not be, for know that our law doth make it treason itself for one of our people to look through a person of royal blood. Oh, no, oh, no, little baron, that may never be!"

"Stay, sweet princess," I urged in gentlest tones, "not so fast. Thou dost not know what I mean by showing thy heart boldly to thy people. Never fear. I will not break the law of the land, and yet they shall look upon the speck within thy heart, and see how small it is and hear what I have to say about it, and thou shalt not even be visible to them."

"O little baron," murmured Crystallina, "if this may only be! I feel they will forgive me. Thou art so wise and thy words carry such strong hope to my poor, heavy heart that I almost"—

"Nay, fair princess," I interrupted, "hope for the best, no more. I am not wise enough to read the future, and from what I know of thy people they seem but little different from mine own. Perchance I may be able to sway them toward my views, and make them cry, 'Long live princess Crystallina!' but I can only promise thee to do my best. Betake thee now to the palace, and scorn not for yet a day or so to take up the golden comb and play the damozel Glow Stone in all humility."

CHAPTER XIII

HOW I SET TO WORK TO UNDO A WRONG THAT HAD BEEN DONE IN THE KINGDOM OF THE MIKKAMENKIES, AND HOW BULGER HELPED.—QUEEN GALAXA'S CONFESSION.—I AM CREATED PRIME MINISTER AS LONG AS SHE LIVES.—WHAT TOOK PLACE IN THE THRONE ROOM.—MY SPEECH TO THE MEN OF GOGGLE LAND AFTER WHICH I SHOW THEM SOMETHING WORTH SEEING.—HOW I WAS PULLED IN TWO DIFFERENT DIRECTIONS AND WHAT CAME OF IT.

The first thing I did after the genuine princess Crystallina had left me was to seek out Doctor Nebulosus and learn from him the exact number of hours before the queen's heart would run down.

As he had just been making an examination, he was able to tell the very minute: it was seventeen hours and thirteen minutes, rather a short time you must confess, dear friends, in which to accomplish such an important piece of business as I had in mind. I then made my way directly to the royal palace and demanded a private audience with the Lady of the Crystal Throne.

With the advice of Sir Amber O'Pake and Lord Cornucore she firmly but graciously refused to receive me, giving as an excuse that the excitement that would be sure to follow an interview with the "Man of Coal"—so the

Mikkamenkies had named me—would shorten her life at least thirteen minutes.

But I was not to be put off in so unceremonious a manner. Sitting down, I seized a pen and wrote the following words upon a piece of glazed silk:—

"*To Galaxa, Queen of the Mikkamenkies, Lady of the Crystal Throne.*

"I, Lord Bulger, a Mikkamenkian Noble, Bearer of this, who was the first to discover that the real princess was not sitting on the steps of the Crystal Throne, demand an audience for my Master Baron Sebastian von Troomp, commonly known as 'Little Baron Trump,' and prompted by him I ask, What are thirteen minutes of thy life, O Queen Galaxa, to the long years of sorrow and disappointment in store for thy royal child?"

Taking this letter in his mouth, Bulger sprang away with long and rapid bounds. In a few minutes he was in the presence of the queen, for the guards had fallen back affrighted as they saw him draw near with his dark eyes flashing indignation. Raising himself upon his hind feet, he laid the letter in Galaxa's hands. The moment she had read it she fell into a swoon, and all was stir and commotion in and round about the palace. I was hastily summoned and the audience chamber cleared of every attendant save Doctor Nebulosus, Sir Amber O'Pake, Lord Cornucore, Lord Bulger, and me.

"Send for the damozel Glow Stone," commanded the queen, and when she had appeared, to the amazement of all saving Bulger and me, Galaxa bade her mount the steps of the Crystal Throne, then, having embraced her most tenderly, the queen spoke these words:—

"O faithful Councillors and wise friends from the upper world, this is the real princess Crystallina, whom I have for all these years wickedly and wrongfully kept from her high state and royal privileges. She was born with a speck in her heart, and I feared that it would be useless to ask my people to accept her as my successor."

"Ay, Lady of the Crystal Throne," exclaimed Lord Cornucore, "thou hast wisely done. Thy people would never have received her as Princess Crystallina, for, being by the laws of our land denied the privilege to look for themselves, they never would have believed that this spot in the princess's heart was but a tiny speck like a single hair crystal in the arm of thy magnificent throne. Therefore, O queen, we counsel thee not to imbitter thy last hours by differences with thy loving subjects."

"My Lord Cornucore," said I with a low bow, "I make bold to raise my voice against thine, and I crave permission from Queen Galaxa to parley with her people."

"Forbid it, royal lady!" cried Sir Amber O'Pake savagely, at which Bulger gave a low growl and showed his teeth.

"Queen Galaxa," I added gravely, "a wrong confessed is half redressed. This fair princess, 'tis true, hath a speck in her heart which ill accords with the name bestowed upon her by thy people. Bid me be master until thy heart runs down, and by the Knighthood of all the Trumps I promise thee that thou shalt have three hours of happiness ere thy royal heart has ceased to beat!"

"Be it so, little baron," exclaimed Galaxa joyfully. "I proclaim thee prime minister for the rest of my life." At these words Bulger broke out into a series of glad barks, and, raising upon his hind legs, licked the queen's hand in token of his gratitude, while the fair princess looked a love at me that was too deep to put into words.

"I had now but a few hours to act. The excitement, so Doctor Nebulosus assured me, would shorten the queen's life a full hour."

It had always been my custom to carry about with me a small but excellent magnifying-glass, a double convex lens, for the purpose of making examinations of minute objects, and also for reading inscriptions too fine to be seen with the naked eye. Hastily summoning a skilful metal worker, I instructed him to set the lens in a short tube and to enclose that tube within another, so that I could lengthen it at my pleasure. Then having called together as many of the head men of the nation as the throne room would hold, I requested Lord Cornucore to inform them of the confession which Queen Galaxa had made; namely, that in reality damozel Glow Stone was princess Crystallina and princess Crystallina was damozel Glow Stone.

They were stricken speechless by this piece of information, but when Lord Cornucore went on to tell the whole story and to explain to them why the queen had practised this deception upon them, they broke out into the wildest lamentation, repeating over and over again in piteous tones,—

"A speck in her heart! A speck in her heart! O dire misfortune! O woful day! She never can be our princess if she hath a speck in her heart!" By this time my arrangements were complete. I had placed the princess Crystallina just outside the door of the throne room where she stood concealed behind the thick hangings, and near her I had stationed Doctor Nebulosus with a large circular mirror of burnished silver in his hand. Calling out in a loud voice for silence, I thus addressed the weeping subjects of Queen Galaxa:—

"O Mikkamenkies, Men of Goggle Land, Transparent Folk, I count myself most happy to be among you at this hour and to be permitted, by your gracious queen, to raise my voice in defence of the unfortunate princess with the speck in her heart. Being of noble birth and an inhabitant of another world, it was lawful for me to look through the sorrowing princess, and I have done it. Yes, Mikkamenkies, I have gazed upon her heart; I have seen the speck within it! Give ear, Men of Goggle Land, and you shall know how that speck came there; for it is not, as you doubtless think, a coal-black spot within that fair enclosure, clearer than the columns of Galaxa's throne. Oh, no, Mikkamenkies, a thousand times no: it is a tiny blemish of reddish hue, a drop of princely blood from the upper world, which I inhabit, and this drop in all these countless centuries has coursed through the veins of a thousand kings, and still kept its roseate glow, still remembered the glorious sunshine which called it into being; and now, Men of Goggle Land, lest you think that for some dark purpose of mine own I speak other than the pure and sober truth, behold, I show you the fair Crystallina's heart, in its very life and being as it is, beating and throbbing with hope and fear comingled. Look and judge for yourselves!" And with this I signalled to those on the outside of the palace to carry out my instructions.

BULGER PARTS HIS MASTER FROM PRINCESS CRYSTALLINA.

In an instant the thick curtains were drawn and the throne room was wrapped in darkness, and at the same moment Doctor Nebulosus, with his mirror, caught the strong, white rays of light and threw them upon Crystallina's body, while I through an opening in the hangings made haste to apply the tube to which the lens had been fitted, and, catching the reflected image of her heart, threw it up in plain and startling view upon the opposite wall of the throne room. Upon seeing how small the speck was and how truthfully I had described it, the Mikkamenkies fell a-weeping for purest joy, and then, as if with one voice, they burst out,—

"Long live the fair princess Crystallina with the ruby speck in her heart! and ten thousand blessings on the head of little Baron Trump and Lord Bulger for saving our land from cruel dissensions!" The people on the outside took up the cry, and in a few moments the whole city was thronged with bands of Queen Galaxa's subjects, singing and dancing and telling of their love for the fair princess with the ruby speck in her heart. I had kept my word—Queen Galaxa would have at least three hours of complete happiness ere her heart ran down.

But suddenly the River of Light began to flicker and dim its flood of brilliant white rays.

Night was coming. Noiselessly, as if by magic, the Mikkamenkies faded from my sight, stealing away in search of beds, and as the gloom crept into the great throne room, some one plucked me gently by the hand and a soft voice whispered,—

"I love! I love thee! Oh, who other than I can tell how I love thee!" and then a grip stronger than that gentle hand seized me by the skirt of my coat and dragged me away slowly, but surely, away, through the darkness, through the gloom, out into the silent streets, ever away until at last that soft voice, choking with a sob, ceased its pleading and gasped, "Farewell, oh, farewell! I dare go no farther!" And so Bulger, in his wisdom, led me on and ever on out of the City of the Mikkamenkies, out upon the Marble Highway!

CHAPTER XIV

BULGER AND I TURN OUR BACKS ON THE FAIR DOMAIN OF QUEEN CRYSTALLINA.—NATURE'S WONDERFUL SPEAKING-TUBE.—CRYSTALLINA'S ATTEMPT TO TURN US BACK.—HOW I KEPT BULGER FROM YIELDING.—SOME INCIDENTS OF OUR JOURNEY ALONG THE MARBLE HIGHWAY, AND HOW WE CAME TO THE GLORIOUS GATEWAY OF SOLID SILVER.

Me, the sorrowing Sebastian, loaded with as heavy a heart as ever a mortal of my size had borne away with him, did the wise Bulger lead along the broad and silent highway, farther and yet farther from the city of the Mikkamenkies, until at last the music of the fountains pattering in their crystal basins died away in the distance and the darkness far behind me. I felt that my wise little brother was right, and so I followed on after, with not a sigh or a syllable to stay him.

But he halted at last, and, as I felt about me, I discovered that I was standing beside one of the richly carved seats that one so often meets with along the Marble Highway. I was quite as foot-weary as I was heart-heavy, and reaching out I touched the spring which I knew would transform the seat into a bed, and clambering upon it with my wise Bulger nestled beside me, I soon fell into a deep and refreshing sleep.

When I awoke and, sitting up, looked back toward Queen Crystallina's capital, I could see the River of Light pouring down its flood of white rays far away in the distance; but only a faint reflection came out to where we had passed the night, and then I knew that my faithful companion had led me to the very uttermost limit of the Mikkamenky domain before he had halted. Yes, sure enough, for, as I raised my eyes, there towering above the bed stood the slender crystal column which marked the end of Goggle Land, and upon its face I read the extract from a royal decree forbidding a Mikkamenky to overstep this limit under pain of incurring the queen's most serious displeasure.

Before me was darkness and uncertainty; behind me lay the fair Kingdom of the Transparent Folk yet in sight, lighted up like a long line of happy homes in which the fires were blazing bright and warm on the hearthstones.

Did I turn back? Did I hesitate? No. I could see a pair of speaking eyes fixed upon me, and could hear a low whine of impatience coaxing me along.

Stooping down, I fastened a bit of silken cord taken from the bed to Bulger's collar and bade him lead the way.

It was a long while before the light of Queen Crystallina's city faded away entirely, and even when it ceased to be of any service in making known to me the grandeur and beauty of the vast underground passage, I could still see it glitter like a silver star away, away behind me.

But it disappeared at last, and then I felt that I had parted forever with the dear little princess with the speck in her heart.

Bulger didn't seem to have the slightest difficulty in keeping in the centre of the Marble Highway, and never allowed the leading string to slack up for a moment.

However, it was by no means a tramp through utter darkness, for the lizards of which I have already spoken, aroused by the sound of my footfalls, snapped their tails and lighted up their tiny flash torches in eager attempts to discover whence the noise proceeded, and what sort of a being it was that had invaded their silent domains. We had covered possibly two leagues when suddenly a low and mysterious voice, as soft and gentle as if it had dropped from the clear, starry heavens of my own beautiful world, reached my ear.

"Sebastian! Sebastian!" it murmured. Before I could stop to think, I uttered a cry of wonder, and the noise of my voice seemed to awaken ten thousand of the tiny living flash lights inhabiting the cracks and crevices of the vast arched corridor, flooding it for a moment or so with a soft and roseate radiance.

"Sebastian! Sebastian!" again murmured the mellow and echo-like voice, coming from the very walls of rock beside me.

Hastily drawing near to the spot whence the words seemed to come, I laid my ear against the smooth face of the rock. Again the same soft-sighing voice pronounced my name so clearly and so close beside me that I reached out to grasp Crystallina's hand, for hers was the voice,—the same low, sweet voice that had told me of her sorrow in the Spectral Garden; but there was no one there. In reaching out, however, I had passed my left hand along the face of the wall, and it had marked the presence of a round smooth opening in its rocky face, an opening about the size of a rain-water pipe in the upper world.

Instantly it flashed upon my mind that through some whim of nature this opening extended for leagues back towards the city of the Mikkamenkies through the miles of solid rock, and opened in the very Throne Room of the Princess Crystallina.

Yes, I was right, for after a moment or so again the same low, sweet voice came through the speaking-tube of nature's own making and fell upon my eager ear.

I waited until it had ceased, and setting my mouth in front of the opening I murmured in strong but gentle tones,—

"Farewell, dear Princess Crystallina. Bulger and the little baron both bid thee a long farewell!" and then raising Bulger in my arms, I bade him weep for his royal friend whom he would never see again.

He gave a long, low, piteous cry, half-whine, half-howl, and then I listened for Crystallina's voice. It was not long in coming.

"Farewell, dear Bulger; farewell, dear Sebastian! Crystallina will never forget you until her poor heart with the speck in it runs down and the Crystal Throne knows her no more." Poor Bulger! It now became my turn to tear him from this spot, for Crystallina's voice, sounding thus unexpectedly in his ears, had aroused all the deep affection which he had so ruthlessly smothered in order to bring his little master to his senses and free him from the charm of Crystallina's grace and beauty. But in vain. All my strength, all my entreaties, were powerless to move him from the place.

Evidently Crystallina had heard me pleading with Bulger and had imagined that now I would waver and stand irresolute.

"Heed dear Bulger's prayer, O beloved," she pleaded, "and turn back, turn back to thy disconsolate Crystallina, whom thou madest so happy for a brief moment! Turn back! Oh, turn back!" Bulger now began to whine and cry most piteously. I felt that something must be done at once, or the most direful consequences might ensue—that Bulger, crazed by the sweet tones of Crystallina's voice, might break away from me and dart away in mad race back to the city of the Mikkamenkies, back to the fair young queen of the Crystal Throne.

It became necessary for me to resort to trick and artifice to save my dear little brother from his own loving heart. Drawing his head up against my body and covering his eyes with my left arm, I quickly unloosened my neckerchief, and thrusting it into this wonderful speaking-tube closed it effectively.

And thus I saved my faithful Bulger from himself, thus I closed his ears to the music of Crystallina's voice; but it was not until after a good hour's waiting that he could bring himself to believe that his beloved friend would speak no more.

After several hours more of journeying along the Marble Highway a speck of light caught my eye, far on ahead, and I redoubled my pace to reach it quickly. I was soon rewarded for my trouble by entering a wonderful chamber, circular in form, with a domed roof. In the centre of this fair temple of the underground world sprang a glorious fountain with a mighty rush of waters which brought with them such a phosphorescence that this vast round chamber was lighted up with a pale yellow light in which the countless crystals of the roof and sides sparkled magnificently.

Here we passed the night, or what I called the night, refreshing ourselves with food which I had brought from the Kingdom of the Mikkamenkies, and drinking and bathing in the wonderful fountain which leaped into the air with a rush and a whir, and filled it with a strange and fitful radiance. Upon awaking both Bulger and I felt greatly refreshed both in body and mind, and we made haste to seek out the lofty portal opening upon the Marble Highway, and were soon trudging along it again. Hour after hour we kept on our feet, for something told me that we could not be far away from the confines of some other domain of this World within a World; and this inward prompting of mine proved to be correct, for Bulger suddenly gave a joyful bark and began to caper about as much as to say,—

"O little master, if thou only hadst my keen scent, thou wouldst know that we are drawing near to human habitations of some kind!"

Sure enough, in a few moments a faint light came creeping in beneath the mighty arches of the broad corridor, and every instant it gathered in strength until now I could see clearly about me, and then all of a sudden I caught sight of the source of this shy and unsteady light. There in front of me towered two gigantic candelabra of carved and chased and polished silver, both crowned with a hundred lights, one on each side of the Marble Highway—not the dull, soft flames of oil or wax, but the white tongues of fire produced by ignited gas escaping from the chemist's retort.

It was marvellous, it was magnificent, and I stood looking up at these great clusters of tongues of flames, spellbound by the glorious illumination thus set in silent majesty at this gateway to some city of the under World.

Bulger's warning growl brought me to myself, but I must end this chapter here, dear friends, and halt to collect my thoughts before I proceed to tell you what I saw after passing this glorious gateway illumined by these two gigantic candelabra of solid silver.

CHAPTER XV

THE GUARDS AT THE SILVER GATEWAY.—WHAT THEY WERE LIKE.—OUR RECEPTION BY THEM.—I MAKE A WONDERFUL DISCOVERY.—THE WORLD'S FIRST TELEPHONE.—BULGER AND I SUCCEED IN MAKING FRIENDS WITH THESE STRANGERS.—A BRIEF DESCRIPTION OF THE SOODOPSIES, THAT IS, MAKE BELIEVE EYES, OR THE FORMIFOLK, THAT IS, ANT PEOPLE.—HOW A BLIND MAN MAY READ YOUR WRITING.

O great Don Fum, Master of all Masters, what do I not owe thee for having made known unto me the existence of this wonderful World within a World! Would that I had been a worker in metal! I would not have passed the glorious portal at which I had halted without having set in deep intaglio upon its silver columns the full name of the most glorious scholar whom the world has ever known. Bulger had warned me that this gateway was guarded, and therefore I entered it cautiously, taking care to peer into the dark corners lest I might be a target for some invisible enemy to hurl a weapon at.

No sooner had I passed the gateway than three curious little beings of about my own height threw themselves swiftly and silently across the pathway. They wore short jackets, knee-breeches, and leggings reaching to their ankles, but no hats or shoes, and their clothes were profusely decorated with beautiful silver buttons.

Their hands and feet and heads seemed much too large for their little bodies and pipe-stemmy legs, and gave them an uncanny and brownie look, which was greatly increased by the staring and glassy expression of their large, round eyes. When I first caught sight of them they had hold of hands, but now they stood each with his pair stretched out toward Bulger and me, waving them strangely in the air and agitating their long fingers as if they were endeavoring to set a spell upon us.

I imagined that I could feel a sensation of drowsiness creeping over me and made haste to call out:—

"Nay, good people, do not strive to set a spell upon me. I am the illustrious explorer from the upper world,—Sebastian von Troomp,—and come to you with most peaceful intent."

But they paid no heed to my words, merely advancing a few inches and with outstretched hands continued to beat and claw the air, pausing only to signal to each other by touching each other's hands or different parts of each other's bodies. I was deeply perplexed by their actions, and took a step or two forward when instantly they fell back the same distance.

"All men are brothers," I exclaimed in a loud tone, "and carry the same shaped hearts in their breasts. Why do you fear me? You are thrice my number and in your own home. I pray you stand fast and speak to me!"

As I was pronouncing these words, they kept jerking their heads back as if the sound of my voice were smiting them in the face. It was very strange. Suddenly one of them drew from his pocket a ball of silken cord, and, deftly unrolling it, tossed one end toward me. It flew directly towards me, for its end was weighed with a thin disk of polished silver, as was the end retained in the hand of the thrower. His next move was to open his jacket and apparently press his disk against his bare body right over his heart. I made haste to do the same with mine, holding it firmly in place. This done, he retreated a step or two until the silken cord had been drawn quite taut. Then he paused and stood for several instants without moving a muscle, after which he passed the disk to one of his companions, who, having pressed it against his heart in turn, passed it to the third of the group.

With the quickness of thought the truth now burst upon me: The three brownie-like creatures in front of me were not only blind, but they were deaf and dumb. The one sense upon which they relied, and which in them was of most marvellous keenness, was the sense of feeling. The strange motions of their hands and fingers, so much like the beating and waving of an insect's feelers, were simply to intercept and measure the vibrations of the air set in motion by the movements of my body. Their large round eyes, too, had but the sense of feeling, but so wondrously acute was it that it was almost like the power of sight, enabling them by the vibration of the air upon the balls to tell exactly how near a moving object is to them. Their purpose in throwing the silken cord and silver disk to me was by measuring the beating of my heart and comparing it with their own to determine whether I was human like them.

Judge of my astonishment, dear friends, upon seeing one of their number point to the silver disk and, by means of sign-language, give me to understand that they wanted to feel the heart of the living creature in my company.

Stooping down, I hastened to gratify their curiosity by applying it over my dear Bulger's heart.

At once there was an expression of most comical amazement depicted on their faces as they passed the disk from one to the other and pressed it against different parts of their bodies—now against their breasts, now against their cheeks, and even against their closed eyelids. Of course I knew that their amazement proceeded from the rapid beating of Bulger's heart, and I enjoyed their child-like surprise very much. All expression of fear now vanished from their faces, and I was delighted with the look of sweet temper and good humor that played about their features, now wreathed in smiles.

Slowly and on tip-toe they drew near to Bulger and me and for several minutes amused themselves mightily by running their long, flexible fingers hither and thither over our bodies.

It did not take them long to discover that I was to all intents and purpose a creature of their own kind, but not so with Bulger. Their round faces became seamed and lined with wonder as they made themselves acquainted with his, to them, strange build, and ever and anon as they felt him over would they pause and in lightning-like motions of their fingers on each other's hands and arms and faces exchange thoughts as to the wonderful being which had entered the portal of their city.

No doubt you are dying of impatience, dear friends, to be told something more definite concerning these strange people among whom I had fallen. Well, know, then, that their existence had been darkly hinted at in the manuscript of the Great Master, Don Fum. I say darkly hinted at, for you must bear in mind that Don Fum never visited this World within a World; that his wonderful wisdom enabled him to reason it all out without seeing it, just as the great naturalists of our day, upon finding a single tooth belonging to some gigantic creature which lived thousands of years ago, are able to draw complete pictures of him.

Well, these curious beings whose city Bulger and I had entered are called by two different names in Don Fum's wonderful book. In some places he speaks of them as the Soodopsies, or Make-believe Eyes, and in others as the Formifolk or Ant People. Either name was most appropriate, their large, round, clear eyes being really make-believe ones, for, as I have told you, they had absolutely no sense of sight; while on the other hand, the fact that they were deaf, dumb, and blind, and lived in underground homes, made them well entitled to the name of Ant People. In a few moments the three Soodopsies had succeeded in teaching me the main principles of their pressure-language, so that I was, to their great delight, enabled to answer a number of their questions.

THE FORMIFOLK TRY THE BEAT OF THE BARON'S HEART BY TELEPHONE.

But think not, dear friends, that these very wise and active little folk, skilled in so many arts, have no other language than one consisting of pressures of different degree, made by their finger-tips upon each other's bodies. They had a most beautiful language, so rich that they were able to express the most difficult thoughts, to give utterance to the most varied emotions; in short, a language quite the equal of ours in all respects save one—it contained absolutely no word that could give them the faintest notion what color was. This is not to be wondered at, for they themselves neither had nor could have even the faintest conception of what I meant by color, so that when I attempted to make them understand that our stars were bright points in the sky, they asked me if they would prick my finger if I should press upon one of them. But you doubtless are anxious to know how the Formifolk can possibly make use of any other language than that of pressures. Well, I will tell you. Every Soodopsy carried at his girdle a little blank-book, if I may so term it, the covers being of thin silver plates variously carved and chased as the owner's taste may prompt. The leaves of this book also consist of thin sheets of silver not much thicker than our tin-foil; also fastened to his girdle by a silken cord hangs a silver pen or, rather, a stylus. Now, when a Soodopsy wishes to say something to one of his people, something too difficult to express by pressures of the finger-tips, he simply turns over a leaf of the silver against the inside of either cover, both of which are slightly padded, and taking up his stylus proceeds to write out what he wishes to say; and this done he deftly tears the leaf out and hands it to his companion, who taking it and turning it over, runs the wonderfully sensitive tips of his fingers over the raised writing and reads it with the greatest ease; only of course he reads from right to left instead of from left to light, as it was written. So, hereafter, when I repeat my conversations with the Formifolk, you will understand how they were conducted.

CHAPTER XVI

IDEAS OF THE FORMIFOLK CONCERNING OUR UPPER WORLD.—THE DANCING SPECTRE.—THEIR EFFORTS TO LAY HOLD OF HIM.—MY SOLEMN PROMISE THAT HE SHOULD BEHAVE HIMSELF.—WE SET OUT FOR THE CITY OF THE MAKE-BELIEVE EYES.—MY AMAZEMENT AT THE MAGNIFICENCE OF THE APPROACHES TO IT.—WE REACH THE GREAT BRIDGE OF SILVER, AND I GET MY FIRST GLANCE OF THE CITY OF CANDELABRA.—BRIEF ACCOUNT OF THE WONDERS SPREAD OUT BEFORE MY EYES.—EXCITEMENT OCCASIONED BY OUR ARRIVAL.—OUR SILVER BED-CHAMBER.

Although thousands and thousands of years had gone by since the Formifolk had, by constant exposure to the flicker and glare of the burning gas which their ancestors had discovered and made use of to illumine their underground world, gradually lost their sense of sight, and then in consequence of the deep and awful silence that forever reigned about them had also lost their sense of hearing and naturally thereafter their power of speech, yet, marvellous to relate, they still kept within their minds dim and shadowy traditions of the upper world, and the "mighty lamp," as they called the sun, which burned for twelve hours and then went out, leaving the world in darkness until the spirits of the air could trim it again. And, strange to say, many of the unreal things of the upper world had been by the workings of their minds transformed into realities, while the realities had become the merest cobwebs of the brain. For instance, the shadows cast by our bodies in the sunlight and forever following at our heels they had come to think were actual creatures, our doubles, so to speak, and that on account of these "dancing spectres," as they called them, which dogged our footsteps for our life long, sitting like mar-joys at our feasts, it was utterly impossible for the people of the upper world to be entirely happy as they were, and it occurred to them at once that I must have such a double following at my heels, so several times they suddenly joined hands, and, forming a circle about me, gradually closed up with intent to lay hold of the dancing spectre. This they did, too, after I had assured them that what they had in mind was the mere shadow cast by a person walking in the light. But as they had absolutely no idea of the nature of light, I only had my trouble for my pains.

Nor did they give over making every now and then the most frantic and laughable efforts to catch the little dancing gentleman who, as they were bound to think, was quietly trudging along at my heels, but who, so they informed me, was far quicker in his motions than any escaping water or falling object. Finally, they held one of their silent but very excited powwows, during which the thousand lightning-like pressures and tappings which they made upon each other's bodies gave the spectator the idea that they were three deaf and dumb schoolboys engaged in a scrimmage over a bag of marbles, and then they informed me that they had resolved to permit Bulger and me to enter their city provided I would give them the word of a nobleman that I would restrain my nimble-footed double from doing them any harm.

I made them a most solemn promise that he should behave himself. Whereupon they greeted both Bulger and me as brothers, stroking our hair, patting our heads, and kissing me on the cheeks, and, what was more, they told us their names, which were Long Thumbs, Square Nose, and Shaggy Brows.

All this time I had been every now and then casting anxious glances on ahead of me, for I was dying of impatience to enter the marvellous city of the Ant People.

I say marvellous, dear friends, for though many had been the wonderful things I had seen in my lifetime in the faraway corners of the upper world, yet here was a sight which, as it gradually unfolded itself before my eyes, shackled my very heart and caused me to gasp for breath. It was with no little surprise at the very outset that I discovered that the walls and floor of the beautiful passage through which the Soodopsies were leading Bulger and me were of pure silver, the former being composed of polished panels ornamented with finely executed chasings and carvings, and the latter, as had in fact all the floors and streets and passages of the city having upon their polished surfaces slightly raised characters which I will explain later. But as one passage opened into another, and then four or more all centred in a vast circular chamber which we traversed with our three silent guides only to enter chambers and corridors of greater size and beauty, all brilliantly lighted by rows of the same glorious candelabra upholding clusters of tongues of flame—I could compare the scene to nothing save a series of magnificent ballrooms and banquet-halls, out of which the happy guests had been suddenly driven by the deep and awful rumble of an earthquake shock, the lights having been left burning.

Now the scene began to change. Long Thumbs, who was leading the way, and in whose large palm my little hand lay completely lost, suddenly turned to the right and led me up an arched way. I saw that we were crossing a bridge over a stream as black and sluggish as Lethe itself.

But such a bridge! Never had my eye rested upon so light and airy a span, springing from bank to bank; not the plain and solid work of the stone-mason, but the fair and cunning result of the metal worker's skill, like the labor of love, delicate, yet strong, and almost too beautiful for use.

Two rows of silver lamps of exquisite workmanship crowned its gracefully arching sides, and when we stood upon its highest bend, Long Thumbs halted and wrote upon his tablet: "Now, little baron, we are about to enter the dwelling-place of our people. Thy head is large, and there is, no doubt, much of wisdom stored away in thy brain. Make such use of it as not to disturb the perfect happiness of our nation, for no doubt many of our people will be suspicious of thee, and for the first time in thousands of years a Soodopsy will lay him down to sleep, and in his dreams feel the touch of the dancing spectre of the upper world." I promised Long Thumbs that he should have no reason to be dissatisfied with me, and then making an excuse that I was a-weary, I feasted my eyes for several moments upon the glorious scene spread out before me.

It was the city of the Formifolk in all its splendor—a splendor, alas, unseen by, unknown to, the very people dwelling in it, for to them its silver walls and arches, its endless rows of glorious candelabra uplifting their countless clusters of never-dying jets of flame, its exquisitely carved and chiselled portals and gateways, its graceful chairs and settees and beds and couches and tables and lamps and basins and ewers and thousands of articles of furniture all in purest silver, hammered or wrought by the cunning hands of their ancestors while they still were possessed of the power of sight, could only be known to these, their descendants, by the sole sense of feeling.

From the lofty ceilings of corridors and archways, from the jutting ornaments of the house-fronts, from cornice and coping, from the four sides of columns, and from the corners of cupolas and minarets, here and there and everywhere hung silver lamps of more than Oriental beauty of form and finish, all with their never-dying tongues of flame sending forth a soft though unsteady light to fall upon sightless eyes!

But yet these countless flames, by the aid of which I was enabled to gaze upon the splendor of this city of silver palaces, were life if not light to the Soodopsies, for they warmed these vast subterranean depths and filled them with a deliciously soft and strangely balmy air.

And yet to think that Bulger and I were the only two living creatures to be able to look upon this scene of almost celestial beauty and radiance!

It made me sad, and plunged me into such a fit of deep abstraction that it required a second gentle tug of Long Thumbs' hand to bring me to myself.

As we crossed the bridge and entered the city proper, I was delighted to note that the streets and open squares were ornamented with hundred of statues all in solid silver, and that they represented specimens of a race of great beauty of person; and then it occurred to me how fortunate it was that the Soodopsies could not gaze upon these images of their ancestors and thus become living witnesses of their own woful falling-away from the former physical grace of their race.

Now, like human ants that they were, the Formifolk began to swarm forth from their dwellings on every side of the city, and my keen ear caught the low shuffling sound of their bare feet over the silver streets as they closed in about us, their arms flashing in the light and their faces lined with strange emotions as they learned of the arrival among them of two creatures from the upper world. They were all clad, men and women alike, in silk garments of a chestnut brown, and I at once concluded that they drew this material from the same sources as the Mikkamenkies, for, dear friends, you must not get an idea that the Formifolk were not well deserving of the name which Don Fum had bestowed upon them. They were genuine human ants and, except when sleeping, always at work.

It was true that since their blindness had come upon them they had not been able to add a single column or archway to the Silver City, but in all the ordinary concerns of life they were quite as industrious as ever, chasing, carving, chiselling, planting, weaving, knitting, and doing a thousand and one things that you and I with our two good eyes would find it hard to accomplish.

I had made known to Long Thumbs the fact that Bulger and I were both very tired and weary from our long tramp, and that we craved to have some refreshment set before us, and then to be permitted to go to rest at once, promising that after we had had several hours' good sleep we would take the greatest pleasure in being presented to the worthy inhabitants of the Silver City.

It was astonishing with what rapidity this request of mine spread from man to man. Long Thumbs made it known to two at the same time, and these two to four, and these four to eight, and these eight to sixteen, and so on. You see it wouldn't take long at that rate to tell a million.

Like magic the Formifolk disappeared from the streets, and in a sort of orderly confusion faded from my sight. Bulger and I were right glad to be conducted to a silver bed-chamber, where the traveller's every want seemed to be anticipated. The only thing that bothered us was, we had not been accustomed to keep the light burning upon going to bed, and this made us both a little wakeful at first; but we were too tired to let it keep us from dropping off after a few moments, for the mattress was soft and springy enough to satisfy any one, and I'm sure that no one could have complained that the house wasn't quiet enough.

CHAPTER XVII

IN WHICH YOU READ, DEAR FRIENDS, SOMETHING ABOUT A LIVE ALARM CLOCK AND A SOODOPSY BATHER AND RUBBER.—OUR FIRST BREAKFAST IN THE CITY OF SILVER.—A NEW WAY TO CATCH FISH WITHOUT HURTING THEIR FEELINGS.—HOW THE STREETS AND HOUSES WERE NUMBERED, AND WHERE THE SIGNBOARDS WERE.—A VERY ORIGINAL LIBRARY IN WHICH BOOKS NEVER GET DOG-EARED.—HOW VELVET SOLES ENJOYED HER FAVORITE POETS.—I AM PRESENTED TO THE LEARNED BARREL BROW, WHO PROCEEDS TO GIVE ME HIS VIEWS OF THE UPPER WORLD.—THEY ENTERTAINED ME AMAZINGLY AND MAY INTEREST YOU.

I can't tell you, dear friends, exactly how long Bulger and I slept, but it must have been a good while, for when I was awakened I felt thoroughly refreshed. I say awakened, for I was awakened by a gentle tapping on the back of my hand—six taps.

At first I thought I was dreaming, but, upon rubbing my eyes, I saw standing by the side of my bed one of the Soodopsies who, feeling me stir, took up his tablet and wrote as follows:—

"My name is Tap Hard. I am a clock. There is a score of us. We keep the time for our people by counting the swing of the pendulum in the Time House. It swings about as fast as we breathe. There are one hundred breaths to a minute and one hundred minutes to an hour. Our day is divided into six hours' worktime and six hours' sleeptime. It is now the rising hour. If thou wilt be pleased to rise, one of our people from the Health House will rub all the tired out of thy limbs."

I touched Tap Hard's heart to thank him, and made haste to scramble out of bed. Now, for the first time, I looked about the silver chamber in which I had slept. On silver shelves lay silver combs and silver shears and silver knives; on a silver stand stood a silver ewer within a silver basin; on silver pegs hung silken towels, while spread upon the silver floor lay soft, silken rugs, and above and around on ceiling and walls the tongues of flame were a thousand times repeated in the panels of burnished silver.

I had made trial of all sorts of Oriental rubber and bath attendants in my day, but the silent little Soodopsy who laved and rubbed and tapped and stroked me exceeded them all in dexterity, added to which was a new charm, for I was not obliged to listen to long and senseless tales of adventure and intrigue, but was left quite alone to my own thoughts. Bulger was also treated to a sponging and a rubbing—a luxury which he had not enjoyed since we had left Castle Trump.

My toilet was no sooner completed than Long Thumbs made his appearance to inquire after my health and to superintend the serving of my breakfast, which consisted of a piece of most delicate boiled fish flanked with oysters of delicious flavor, and trimmed with slices of those monstrous mushrooms which I had eaten among the Mikkamenkies, the whole served in a beautiful silver dish on a silver tray with silver eating utensils.

Remembering the strange way in which the fish were caught and killed in the Land of the Mikkamenkies, I was curious to know how the Soodopsies managed it, for I knew enough of them to know that the sensation of anything struggling for its life in their hands would suffice to throw them into fits of great suffering, to fill their gentle hearts with nameless terror.

"At the end of one of the many corridors leading out of our city," explained Long Thumbs, "there is a rocky chamber which was called by our ancestors Uphaslok, or the Death Hole, because any being which breathes its air for a few moments is sure to die. So they closed it up forever, leaving only a small pipe projecting through the door; but, strange to say, those who breathe this air suffer no pain whatever, but presently drop off into a pleasant dream, and, unless they be rescued, would, of course, never wake again. Now, as our laws forbid us to cause any pain to the most insignificant creature, it occurred to our ancestors that by means of a long pipe they could turn this poisoned air into the river whenever they wanted a supply of fish for food. This they did, and, strange to say, the moment the fish felt the gas bubbling into the river, they at once swam up to the mouth of the pipe, and struggled with each other for a chance to catch the deadly bubbles as they left its mouth, so pleasant a sensation do they cause as they gradually plunge, the creature breathing them into his last sleep. And in this way it is we are enabled to feed upon the fish in our river, without breaking the law of the land."

I began to understand that I had fallen in with a very original and interesting folk, but Bulger was not altogether pleased with them, for several reasons, as I soon observed. In the first place he couldn't accustom himself to the cold and glassy look of their eyes, and in the next he was a bit jealous of their wonderfully keen scent—a sense which with them was so strong that they invariably gave signs of being conscious of Bulger's approach even before I could see him, and always turned their faces in the direction in which he was coming.

You will remember, dear friends, that I mentioned the fact that the Formifolk went barefoot, and that their feet as well as their hands seemed altogether too large for their bodies, and I wish to add, that while Bulger and I were being led through the long corridors and winding passages on our way into the City of Silver, the three Soodopsies frequently half halted and seemed to be feeling on the floor for something with the balls of their feet. I thought no more about it, until Bulger and I started out for our first stroll through their wonderful town, when, to my great delight, I made the discovery that the numbers of the houses, the names of the occupants, the names of the streets, as well as all signboards, so to speak, and all guide-posts were in slightly raised letters on the floors and pavements, and then the truth dawned upon me, that Long Thumbs and his companions were simply halting now and then to read the names of the streets with the balls of their feet, in order to know if they were taking the right road.

BARREL BROW ENGAGED IN READING FOUR BOOKS AT ONCE.

Ay, more than this, dear friends, the first time Bulger and I passed through one of the open squares of the City of Silver, you may imagine my satisfaction upon the discovery that the silver pavements were literally covered with the writings of the Soodopsy authors in raised characters.

Now, in Don Fum's wonderful book he had, in his masterly manner, given me the key to the language of the Formifolk, so that with very slight effort I was able to make the additional discovery that some of the streets were given up to the writers of history, and some to story writers, while others were filled with the learned works of philosophers, and others still contained many thousands of lines from the best poets which the nation had produced.

And I had very little difficulty in discovering which were the favorite poems of the Soodopsies, for, as you may readily suppose, these were polished like a silver mirror by the shuffling of the many thankful feet over their sweet and soulful lines.

I noticed that the writings of the philosophers in this, as in my own world, found few readers, for the raised letters were, in many cases, tarnished and black from lack of soles trampling over them in search of wisdom.

Somewhat later, when I had become acquainted with Velvet Soles, the daughter of Long Thumbs, a gracious little being as full of inward light as she was blind to the outer world, and she invited me to "come for a read," I had a hard task of it in persuading her that I could not remove what she called my ridiculous "foot boxes" and join her in enjoying some of her favorite poems. It was to me a delicious pastime to accompany this happy little maiden when she "went for a read," to walk beside her and watch the ever-varying expression of her beautiful face as the soles of her tiny feet pressed the words of love and hope and joy, and her heart expanded, and she clasped her hands in attitudes of blissful enjoyment, seemingly just as deep and fervent as if the blessed sunlight rested on her brow, and her eyes were drinking in the glory of a summer sunset. O dwellers in the upper world with the light streaming into the windows of your souls, with your ears open to the music of pipe and flute and violin, and to the sweeter music of the voice of love, how much more have ye than she, and yet how rarely are ye as happy, how rarely do ye know that sweet contentment which, as in this case, came from within?

"Go to the ant; consider her ways, and be wise, which, having no guide, overseer, or ruler, provideth her meat in the summer and gathereth her food in the harvest."

In a short time the Formifolk seemed to become quite accustomed to having Bulger and me among them, and they apparently "touched hands" with me in quite as friendly a fashion as if I had been one of them.

One day Long Thumbs conducted me to the house of the most aged and learned of the Soodopsies, Barrel Brow by name.

He received me very cordially, although I interrupted him at his studies, for, as I entered his apartment, he was in the act of reading four different books at the same time: two were lying on the floor, and he was perusing their raised characters with the soles of his feet, and two others were set up on a frame in front of him and he was deciphering them with the tips of his fingers.

But when informed who I was he stopped work at once and taking up his tablets, asked me a number of questions concerning the upper world, of which he had, however, no very exalted opinion.

"You people," said he, "if I understand correctly the ancient writings of those of our nation who still preserved certain traditions of the upper world, are endowed with several senses which are utterly lacking in us, I am happy to say, for if I understand correctly ye have in the first place a sense which ye call hearing, a most troublesome sense, for by means of it ye are being constantly disturbed and annoyed by vibrations of the air coming from afar. Now, they can be of no possible good to you. Ye might as well have a sense that would inform you what was going on in the moon. Therefore, my conclusion is, that the sense of hearing only serves to distract and weaken the brain.

"Another sense that ye are possessed of," continued Barrel Brow, "ye call the sense of sight—a power even more useless and distracting than hearing, for the reason that it enables you to know things which it is utterly bootless to know, such as what your next door neighbors may be doing, how the mountains are acting on the other side of your rivers, how your sky, as ye call it, might feel if you could touch it with your fingers, which ye can't do, however; how soon rain will fall, which is a useless piece of knowledge if ye have roofs to cover you, as I suppose ye have; but the most ridiculous use which ye make of this sense of sight is the manufacture of what ye call pictures, by means of which ye seem to take the greatest pleasure in deceiving this very sense of which ye are so very proud. If I understand correctly these pictures, if felt of, are quite as smooth as that panel there, but so cunningly do ye draw the lines and lay in the colors, whatever they may be, that ye really succeed in deceiving yourselves and stand for hours in front of one of these bits of trickery when ye might, if ye chose, feast your eyes, as ye call it, upon the very thing which the trickster has imitated. Now, as life is much shorter in the upper world than in ours, it seems very strange to me that ye should wish to waste it in this foolish manner. Then, there is another thing, little baron," continued the learned Barrel Brow, "which I wish to mention. It is this: The people of the upper world pride themselves very much upon what they term the power of speech, which, if I understand correctly, is a faculty they have of expressing their thoughts to each other by violently expelling the air from their lungs, and that this air, rushing into the ventilators of the brain, which ye call ears, produces a sensation of sound as ye term it, and in this way one of thy people standing at one end of the town might make his wishes known to another standing at the other end. Now, thou wilt pardon my thinking so, little baron, but this seems to me to be not a whit above the brute creature, which, opening its vast jaws, thus sets the air in motion in calling its young or breathing defiance at an enemy. And if I understand correctly, little baron, so proud are thy people of this power of speech that they insist upon making use of it at all times and upon all occasions, and, strange to say, these 'talkers' can always find plenty of people to open their ears to these vibrations of the air, although the effect is so wearying to the brain that in the end they invariably fall asleep. But if I understand correctly, the women are even fonder of displaying their skill in thus puffing out the air from their lungs than the men are; but, that not satisfied with this superior power of puffing out the words, they actually have recourse to a potent herb which they steep in boiling water and drink as hot as possible on account of its effect in loosening the tongue and allowing the talker to do more puffing than she could otherwise.

"But all this, little baron," continued the learned Barrel Brow, "might be overlooked and regarded in the light of mere amusement were it not for the fact, if I understand correctly, that brain ventilators being of different sizes in different persons, the consequence is that these puffs of air which ye use to make known your thoughts to each other produce different effects upon different persons, and the result is, that the people of the upper world spend half their time repeating the puffs which they have already sent out, and that even then thou canst rarely find two people who will agree exactly as to the number, kind, strength, and meaning of the puffs blown into each other's brain ventilators, and that therefore has it become necessary to provide what ye call judges to settle these disputes which often last for lifetimes, the two parties spending their entire fortunes hiring witnesses to come before these judges and imitate the sound which the air made when it was set in motion years ago by the angry puffs of the two parties. I sincerely trust, little baron," wrote the learned Barrel Brow on his tablet of silver, "that when thou returnest to thy people thou wilt make known to them what I have written for thee to-day, for it is never too late to correct a fault, and the longer that fault has lasted the greater the credit for correcting it."

I promised the learned Soodopsy to do as he requested, and then we touched each other on the back of the head, which is the way they say good-by in the land of the Formifolk, a touch on the forehead meaning, "How d'ye do?"

CHAPTER XVIII

EARLY HISTORY OF THE SOODOPSIES AS RELATED BY BARREL BROW.—HOW THEY WERE DRIVEN TO TAKE REFUGE IN THE UNDER WORLD, AND HOW THEY CAME UPON THE MARBLE HIGHWAY.—THEIR DISCOVERY OF NATURAL GAS WHICH YIELDS THEM LIGHT AND WARMTH, AND OF NATURE'S MAGNIFICENT TREASURE HOUSE.—HOW THEY REPLACED THEIR TATTERED GARMENTS AND BEGAN TO BUILD THE CITY OF SILVER.—THE STRANGE MISFORTUNES THAT CAME UPON THEM, AND HOW THEY ROSE SUPERIOR TO THEM, TERRIBLE AS THEY WERE.

And, no doubt, dear friends, you would be glad to hear something about the early history of the Soodopsies: who they were, where they came from, and how they happened to find their way down into the World within a World.

At least, this was the way I felt after I had been presented to the learned Barrel Brow, and so the next time I called upon him I waited patiently for him to finish reading the four books in front of him, and then I said,—

"Be pleased, dear Master, to tell me something concerning the early history of thy people, and to explain to me how they came to make their way down into this underground world."

"Ages and ages ago," wrote the learned Barrel Brow, "my people lived upon the shores of a beautiful land with a vast ocean to the north of it, and in those days they had the same senses as the other people of the upper world. It was a very fair land, indeed, so fair that, in the words of the ancient chronicles, the sun looked in vain for a fairer. Its rivers were deep and broad, its plains were rich and fertile, and its mountains stored full of silver and gold and copper and tin, and so easily mined were these metals that our people became famous as metal workers; so deft in their workmanship that the other nations from far and near came to us for swords and shields and spear heads and suits of armor and table service and armlets and bracelets and, above all, for lamps most gloriously chased and carved to hang in their palaces and temples. And so we were very happy, until one terrible day the great round world gave a twist and we were turned away from the sun, so that its rays went slantingly over our heads and gave us no warmth.

"Ah me, I could weep now," exclaimed the learned Barrel Brow, "after all these centuries, when I think of the cruel fate that overtook my people. In a few months the whole face of our fair land was covered with ice and snow, and our cattle died, and many of our people, too, before they could weave thick cloth to keep their delicate bodies from the pinching cold. But this was not all; the great blue ocean which had until then dashed its warm waves and white foam up against our shores now breathed its icy breath full upon us, driving into our cellars to escape its fury; and in a few brief months, to our horror, there came drifting down upon us fields and mountains of ice, which the tempestuous waters cast up against our shores with deafening crash. To remain there meant death, swift and terrible, so the command was given to abandon homes and firesides and escape to the southward, and this most of them did. But it so happened that several hundred families belonging to the metal-working guilds, who knew the underground passages to the mines as foresters know the pathless wood, had taken refuge in the vast underground caverns with all the goods they could carry. Poor deluded creatures! they thought that this sudden coming of the winter blast, of the blinding snow and vast floating fields of ice, was but a freak of nature, and that in a few months the old warmth and the old sunshine would come back again.

"Alas, months went by and their supply of food was almost exhausted and the entrances to the mines were closed by gigantic blocks of ice cemented into one great mass by the snow which the gray clouds had sifted down upon them. There was now no escape that way. Their only hope was to make their way underground to some portal to the upper world.

"So, with lighted torches but with hearts plunged in the darkness of despair, they kept on their way, when one day, or one night, they knew not which, their leaders suddenly came upon a broad street of marble opened by nature's own hands. It was skirted by a softly flowing river that swarmed with fish in scales and shells and skin, and here our people halted to eat and drink and rest, and while one of their number was striking his flint on one occasion to make a fire to cook a meal, to his surprise and delight a tongue of flame darted up from the rocky floor and continued to burn, giving light and warmth to them.

"As they had brought their tools—their drills and chisels and files and gravers and blow-pipes—with them in their carts and wagons, they made haste to fit a pipe to this opening in the rock and set up a cluster of lights. With food and water and warmth and light their hearts grew lighter, especially as they soon discovered that in many of the vast caverns gigantic mushrooms grew in the wildest profusion.

"The wisest of them," continued the learned Barrel Brow, "at once made up their minds that there must be reservoirs of this gas farther along on this beautiful Marble Highway, so, day by day, they pushed farther into this World within a World, halting every now and then to set up a lighthouse as they called it.

"After advancing several leagues the exploring party, upon lighting a cluster of gas jets, were stricken almost speechless with wonder at finding themselves upon the very sill of a towering portal opening into a succession of vast chambers, some with flat ceiling, some arched, some domed, upon the floors and walls of which lay and hung inexhaustible quantities of pure silver. Those magnificent caverns were in reality nature's vast storehouses of the glorious white metal, and our people made haste to set up clusters of gas jets here and there, so that they might view the wondrous treasure-house.

"Here they determined to remain, for here was food and water in never-failing supplies, and here they would have light and warmth, and here they could forget their miseries by working at their calling, using the precious metal with lavish hand to build them living-chambers, and to fashion the thousand and one things necessary for every-day life. So great was their delight as metal-workers to come upon this exhaustless supply of pure silver that they could hardly sleep until they had set up clusters of gas jets throughout these vast caverns, for, no doubt, little baron, thou hast already guessed that this is the spot I am telling thee of; that right here it was where our people halted to build the City of Silver.

"But one thought troubled them and that was where to find needful clothing, for the old was fast falling into shreds and tatters, when, to their delight, they came upon a bed of mineral wool and with this they managed to weave some cloth. Although it was rather stiff and harsh, yet it was better than none.

"While exploring a new cavern one day, one of my wise ancestors saw a large night moth alight near him, and, gently loosening some of its eggs, he carried them home, more as a curiosity than aught else.

"Imagine how rejoiced he was, however, to see one of the worms which hatched out set to work spinning a cocoon of silk half as big as his fist. There was great feasting and merry-making among our people upon hearing of this glad news, and it was not very long before many a silver shuttle was rattling in a silver loom, and the soft bodies of our people were warmly and comfortably clad. Now, long periods of time went by, which, cut up into your months, would have made many, many years. Our people had everything but sunlight, and this, of course, those who were born in the under world knew nothing about and therefore did not miss.

"But, as was to be expected, great changes gradually took place in our people. To their inexpressible grief, they noticed that as they busied themselves beautifying their new homes by erecting arches and bridges and terraces, and lining them with glorious candelabra and statues, all in cast and wrought or hammered silver, their sight was gradually failing them, and that in not a very great length of time they should be totally blind.

"This result, little baron," continued the learned Barrel Brow, "was very natural, for the sense of sight was in reality created for sunlight; for as thou no doubt knowest, all the fish that swim in our rivers have no eyes, having no need of them. It happened just as they had expected—in a few generations more our people discovered that their eyes could no longer see things as thou dost, but yet they could feel them if they were not too far away, just as I can feel thy presence now and tell where thou sittest, and how tall thou art, and how broad thou art, and whether thou movest to right or left, forward or backward, but I cannot tell exactly how thou art made until I reach out and touch thee; then I know all; yes, far better than thou canst know, for our sense of feeling is keener than thy so-called sight. One of my people can feel a grain or roughness upon a silver mirror which to thy eyes seems smoother than glass. Well, strange to relate, and yet not strange, our ancestors with the going-out of their sense of sight also felt their sense of hearing on the wane. Our ears, as thou callest them, having nothing more to listen to, for eternal silence, as thou knowest, reigns in this under world, became as useless to us as the tail of the pollywog would be to the full-grown frog; and of course with the loss of our sense of hearing our children were soon unable to learn to talk, and in a certain lapse of time we came to merit full well our new name of Formifolk, or Ant People, for we were now blind and deaf and dumb.

A SOODOPSY MAIDEN READING HER FAVORITE POET

"It is long, very, very long, little baron," continued the learned Soodopsy, "since all recollection of sunlight, of color, of sound, died out of our minds. To-day my people don't even know the names of these things, and thou wouldst have as much chance of success wert thou to attempt to tell them what light or sound is as thou wouldst have if thou shouldst try to explain to a savage that there is nothing under the world to hold it up, and yet it doesn't fall. But if thou shouldst lay several pieces of metal in a row and ask one of my people to tell thee what they were, he would try the weight of each and feel its grain carefully, possibly smell them or touch his tongue to them, and then he would make answer: 'That is gold; that is silver; that is copper; that is lead; that is tin; that is iron.'

"But thou wouldst say, 'They all are differently colored; canst not perceive that?'

"'I know not what thou meanest by color,' he would reply. 'But mark me: now I hide them all beneath this silken kerchief, and still by touching them with my finger tips I can tell what metal each one is. If thou canst do it, then art thou as good a man as I.'

"What sayest now, little baron?" asked the learned Barrel Brow, while his face was wreathed in a smile of triumph; "dost think thou wouldst be as good a man as this Soodopsy?"

"Nay, indeed I do not, wise Master," wrote I upon my silver tablet; "and I thank thee for all thou has told me and taught me, and I ask leave, O Barrel Brow, to come again and converse with thee."

"That thou mayest, little baron," traced the learned Soodopsy upon his silver tablet; and then as I turned to leave his chamber he reached quickly after me and touched me with a bent forefinger, which meant return.

"Thy pardon, little baron," he wrote, "but thou art leaving my study without thy faithful Bulger; am I not right?"

I was astounded, for indeed he was right, and though without the sense of sight he had seen more than I with two good eyes wide open. There lay Bulger fast asleep on a silken-covered hassock.

Our silent conversation had so wearied him that he had sailed off into the Land of Nod on the wings of a dream.

He hung his head and looked very shame-faced when my call aroused him and he discovered that I had actually reached the doorway without his knowing it.

CHAPTER XIX

BEGINS WITH SOMETHING ABOUT THE LITTLE SOODOPSIES, BUT BRANCHES OFF ON ANOTHER SUBJECT; TO WIT;—THE SILENT SONG OF SINGING FINGERS, THE FAIR MAID OF THE CITY OF SILVER.—BARREL BROW IS KIND ENOUGH TO ENLIGHTEN ME ON A CERTAIN POINT, AND HE TAKES OCCASION TO PAY BULGER A VERY HIGH COMPLIMENT, WHICH, OF COURSE, HE DESERVED.

The longer I stayed among the Soodopsies the more did I become convinced that they were the happiest, the lightest hearted, the most contented human beings that I had met in all my travels. If it were possible for the links of a long chain suspended over a chasm to be living, thinking beings for a short while, it seems to me they would hang together in the most perfect accord, for each link would discover that he was no better than his neighbor, and that the welfare of all the other links depended upon him and his upon theirs. So it was with the Formifolk, having no sense of sight they knew no such thing as envy, and all hands were alike when reached out for a greeting.

I was amazed at times to see how they could feel my approach when I would be ten or fifteen feet away from them, and I often amused myself by trying to steal by one of them in the street. But no, it was impossible; a hand would invariably be held out for a greeting. Little by little, they got over their distrust of me, and made up their minds that I had told them the truth when I said that no dancing spectre was forever following at my heels. One of the most interesting sights was to see a group of Soodopsy children at play, building houses with silver blocks, or playing a game very much like our dominoes. I noticed that they kept no tally, such wonderful memories had they that it was quite unnecessary.

At first the children were so frightened upon feeling of me that they fled with terror pictured upon their little faces. Their parents explained to me that I made very much the same impression upon them as if I should feel of a person whose skin was as rough as a sea urchin's.

When at last I succeeded in coaxing several of them to my side, I was astounded to see one little fellow who had by chance pressed his tiny hand against my watch pocket spring away from me terror-stricken. He had felt it tick and didn't stop running until he had reached his mother's side.

His wonderful tale that the little baron carried some strange animal around in his pocket soon caused a crowd to collect about me, and it was some time before I could persuade even the parents that the watch was not alive and that it was not the little animal's heart which they felt beating.

On one occasion, when a little Soodopsy was sitting on my lap with its tiny arm twined affectionately around my neck, I happened to make some remark to Bulger, when, to my amazement, the child sprang out of my arms and darted away with a look of terror upon his little face.

What had I done to him?

Why, it seems that by the merest chance his tiny hand had been pressed against my throat, and that he had been terrified by feeling the strange vibration caused by my voice. Immediately the report was spread about that the little baron carried another little baron around in his throat, that any one could feel him, if I would only consent. It took me a long while to convince them that what they felt was not another little baron, but merely the vibration caused by my expelling my breath in a way peculiar to the people of the upper world. But all the same, I was obliged to say many hundreds of useless things to Bulger in order to give their little hands a chance to feel something so wonderful.

From the little I have told you about the names of the Formifolk, dear friends, you have no doubt understood that their names took their rise from some physical quality, defect, or peculiarity. Besides the names I have already mentioned, I remember Sharp Chin, Long Nose, Silk Ears, Smooth Palms, Big Knuckle, Nail Off, Hammer Fist, Soft Touch, Hole-in-Cheek, or Hole-in-chin (Dimple), Crooked Hair (Cowlick), and so on, and so on.

But, to my amazement, one day, when asking the name of a young girl whose long and delicate fingers had attracted my attention, I was informed that her name was Singing Fingers, or, possibly, I might translate it Music Fingers.

I had noticed that the Soodopsies had some idea of music, for the children often amused themselves dancing, and, while so engaged, beat time with their finger tips on each other's cheeks or foreheads.

But I was completely in the dark as to what they meant by Singing Fingers, or why the young girl should have been so named; hence was I greatly pleased to hear the maiden's mother ask me whether I would like to feel one of her daughter's songs, as she termed it. Upon my acquiescing, the mother approached me and proceeded to roll up the sleeves of my coat until she had laid my arms bare to the elbow, then she took my arms and clasped them across my breast one above the other.

Bulger watched the proceeding with somewhat of displeasure in his eyes; he had half an idea that these silent people might play some hurtful trick upon his little master. But my smile soon disarmed his suspicion.

Singing Fingers now drew near, and as her sweet face with its sightless eyes turned full upon me I could hardly keep back the tears.

And yet, why grieve for any one who seemed to be so perfectly happy? A smile played around her dainty little mouth, disclosing her tiny silvery white teeth like so many real pearls, and her bosom rose and fell quickly, sending forth a faint breathing sound. She looked so like a radiant child of some other world that before I thought, I cried out,—

"Speak, Oh, speak, beautiful child!"

In an instant she drew back affrighted, for the sudden vibration of the air had startled her; but I reached out and touched her hand to give her to understand that she need fear nothing, and then she drew near to me again. Suddenly her beautiful hands with their long, frail, delicate fingers were lifted into the air, and she began to sway her body and to wave her hands in gentle and graceful motions as if keeping time with some music. Gradually she drew nearer to me, and ever and anon her silken finger tips touched my hands or arms as if they were a keyboard and she was about to begin to execute a soft and dainty bit of music; and I noticed that her fingers had some delightful perfume upon them. Now fast and faster the gentle taps rain upon me with rhythmic regularity. They soothe me, they thrill me, they reach my heart as if they were the sweet notes of a flute or the soft tones of a singer's voice. The maiden is really singing to me! It seems to me that I can understand what she is saying, or, rather, thinking, as her dainty finger tips fairly fly hither and thither, and I can hear her low breathing grow louder and louder. Suddenly she leaves my hands and arms and I feel her gentle tapping on my cheeks and brow. So gently, Oh, so gently and soothingly her fingers touch me that at last they feel like rose leaves dragged across my face. The sensation is so delightful, so like the soft touch of sleep to weary eyes, that I drop off in good earnest, and when, after a moment or so, I opened my eyes there sat the smiling Formifolk waiting for me to awake, and there stood the radiant-visaged Singing Fingers in front of me, child-like, waiting to be commended.

And so you see, dear friends, that it is not so hard to be happy after all if you only set about it in the right way. The Formifolk seemed to have set about it in the right way, judging by results, and they are the only things we have to judge by. Some men will fish all day and not have a bite, and some people will try their whole lives to catch happiness and not get any more than a nibble. They don't use the right kind of bait. Let 'em try a kind act, a live one.

There was something I wanted to ask of the learned Barrel Brow, so the next call I made on him I put this question to him:—

"Is it possible, learned Master, that thy people have absolutely no guide, no overseer, no rulers?"

The great scholar of the Formifolk ceased reading the four books which lay opened before him—one under each hand and one under each foot—as I handed him my silver tablet.

"Little baron," was his reply, "if there were only a bramble bush big enough for all you people of the upper world to jump into and if you could only get rid of your ears too, you would soon be rid of your rulers who oppress you, who prey upon you; for no one would have any desire to be a ruler if there was no one left to look at him and if he couldn't hear what the flatterers said about him. Vanity is the soil that rulers spring from, as the mushrooms spring from the rich loam of our dark caverns. They pretend that it is the exercise of power that they are so fond of. Believe them not. It is the gratification of their vanity and nothing else.

"If it were only in thy power to say to every man who itched to be a ruler,—

"'Well and good, brother, a ruler thou shalt be; but bear in mind, weak man, that when thou hast donned thy gaudy uniform and mounted thy gayly caparisoned steed, when thou ridest at the head of troop and cavalcade with ten thousand armed men following thee on foot, as slaves their master, and the plaudits of the foolish multitude rend the air, no eye shall witness the splendor of thy triumph, no ear catch a sound of the deafening cheers,' take my word for it, little baron, no one would want to be a ruler any more.

"Where there are no rulers, little baron," continued the learned Barrel Brow, "there can be no followers; where there are no followers, there will be no quarrelling. When it becomes necessary in our nation we form the Great Circle for deliberation. Each man writes out what he thinks on his tablet. Then the opinions are read and counted and the majority rules. But we form the Great Circle only in times of urgent need. Generally speaking, the smaller circles answer all the purposes; in fact, the family circle is in most cases quite sufficient."

I touched first Barrel Brow's heart in token of my gratitude for the many things which he had taught me, and then the back of his head to bid him good-night. You may imagine his and my delight, dear friends, when the wise Bulger raised himself upon his hind legs, and with his right paw also thanked the learned Barrel Brow, and then bade him good-night by a light tap on the back of his head.

"Fortunate the traveller," wrote the learned Soodopsy, "attended by so wise and watchful a companion! True, like a child, he goes on all fours, but by so doing he brings his heart and his brains on the same level—the only way for a man to wear them if he would do his fellow-creatures any good. The trouble with thy people in the upper world, little baron, is that they think too much. They clasp minds instead of clasping hands; they send messengers with gifts instead of giving themselves. They hire people to dance for them, to sing for them, to be merry for them. They will not be satisfied until they have hired people to help them be sorry, to whom they may say, 'My friend is dead; I loved him. Weep three whole days for him.'"

CHAPTER XX

THIS IS A LONG AND A SAD CHAPTER.—IT TELLS HOW DEAR, GENTLE, POUTING-LIP WAS LOST, AND HOW THE SOODOPSIES GRIEVED FOR HIM AND WHOM THEY SUSPECTED.—BULGER GIVES A STRIKING PROOF OF HIS WONDERFUL INTELLIGENCE WHICH ENABLES ME TO CONVINCE THE SOODOPSIES THAT MY "DANCING SPECTRE" DID NOT CAUSE POUTING-LIP'S DEATH.—THE TRUE TALE OF HIS TERRIBLE FATE.—WHAT FOLLOWS MY DISCOVERY.—HOW A BEAUTIFUL BOAT IS BUILT FOR ME BY THE GRATEFUL SOODOPSIES, AND HOW BULGER AND I BID ADIEU TO THE LAND OF THE MAKE-BELIEVE EYES.

'Twas the custom in the City of Silver to "touch all around," as it was called, before going to rest. The "touch all around" began in a certain quarter of the city and passed with wonderful rapidity from man to man. Exactly how it was done I never could understand, but the purpose of the mysterious signalling was to make an actual count of all the Formifolk. If a single one were missing, it would be most surely discovered by the time the "touch all around" had been completed. It proceeded with lightning-like rapidity throughout the city, and then, if no return signal was made, the people knew that everyone was in his proper place; that no Soodopsy had lost his way or fallen ill in some unfrequented passage.

I don't think that I had more than dropped off to sleep when I was aroused by Bulger's gentle tugging at my sleeve. Rubbing my eyes, I sat up in bed and listened. Instantly my ear caught that faint, shuffling sound which was always perceptible when any number of the Formifolk were hurrying hither and thither over the polished silver pavement.

I sprang out of bed and rushed to the door, Bulger close at my heels. What a strange sight confronted me! I could compare it to nothing save to the appearance of a large ant hill when some mischievous boy suddenly drops a stone among the crowd of petty, patient, plodding people peacefully pursuing their work.

In an instant all is changed: lines are broken, workmen jostle workmen, order becomes disorder, regularity is changed to confusion. Hither and thither the affrighted creatures rush with waving feelers, seeking for the cause of the mad outburst of terror.

So it was with the Formifolk as I looked out upon them. With outstretched hands and tremulously moving fingers they rushed from side to side, jostling and bumping one another, while a nameless dread was depicted upon their upturned faces. Anon a group would halt, join hands, and begin to exchange thoughts by lightning-like pressures, tappings, and strokes, when others would dash against them, break them apart, and confusion would reign greater than ever.

But gradually I noted that some sort of order seemed to be coming out of the movements of this mad throng. Here and there groups of three and four would form and clasp hands, then these smaller circles would break and form into larger ones, and I noted too that this ever-increasing circle was formed on the outside of the panic-stricken crowd, and as it grew it shut them in so that when a fleeing Soodopsy hurtled up against this steady line, his terror left him at once and he took his place in it. In a few moments the madly pushing, jostling throng had disappeared entirely and the whole city was girt round about by these long, steady lines.

The Great Circle had been formed.

After half an hour the deliberation was completed, and, to my surprise, the Great Circle broke up into squads and companies of fours and sixes and tens, and then each disappeared slowly and steadily with lock step, passing out of the City into the dark or only partially lighted chambers and passages that surrounded it. The search for the missing Soodopsy had been begun.

THE GIGANTIC TORTOISE THAT DEVOURED POUTING LIP.

It was hours before the last squad had returned to the square and the Great Circle had been formed again. Alas! the news was sad indeed. There came no tidings of the missing man. He was lost forever; and with clasped hands and slow and heavy step the grieving Formifolk made their way back to their homes, where the sighing women and children were awaiting their coming. As Bulger and I went back to bed again, it almost seemed to me as if I could hear at times the deep and long-drawn sighs that escaped from the gentle breasts of the sorrowing Soodopsies. I noticed a very touching thing on the following day. It was that every man, woman, and child in the City of Silver grieved for the lost Soodopsy as if he were actually brother to each of them. Love was not as with us, in the upper world, a thing bestowed upon those in whom we see our own faces repeated and in whose voices we heard our own ring out again, sweet and clear as in our childhood; in other words, a love almost of our very selves. Oh, no! while it was true that a mother's touch was most tender to her own child, yet no little hand stretched out to her went without its caress. She was mother to them all; to her they were all beautiful, and as their little frocks were all woven in the same loom, there never could come into her mind a temptation to feel whether a rich neighbor's child was playing with hers, and that therefore it ought to receive a more loving caress. In that portion of the city where the children had their playgrounds the silver pavement was in some places marked off with raised lines and letters, something after the manner of our hop scotch, for the purpose of a game which was very popular with the little Soodopsies. Its name is hard to translate, but it meant something like "Little Bogyman," and many an hour had Bulger and I stood there watching these silent little gnomes at play, fascinated by the wonderful skill which they would display in feigning the drawing near of the Little Bogyman, their hiding from him, his stealthy approach, the increasing danger, the attack, the escape, the new dangers, wild flight, and mad pursuit. Fancy, therefore, my astonishment one morning to note that Bulger was coaxing me thither, although the place was quite deserted, the children being all at their lessons.

But, as it was a rule of mine always to humor Bulger's whims, I went patiently along.

In a moment, as we came to the spot where the pavement was marked off and inscribed as I have explained, he halted and with an anxious whine began to play the game of "The Little Bogyman," turning every now and then to see what effect his actions had upon me.

He made no mistakes. As he entered each compartment, he rested his paw upon the raised letters as he had so often seen the children do with their little bare feet, and then mimicked with wonderful fidelity their actions, beginning with the first scent of danger and ending with mad terror at the close pursuit of the bogyman.

I was more than surprised; I was bewildered by this piece of mimicry on Bulger's part. To my mind it boded some terrible accident to him, for I have a superstitious notion that great danger to an animal's life gives him for the moment an almost human intelligence. It is nature caring for her own.

But all of a sudden the real truth in this case burst upon me: it was not my dear little brother giving me to understand that some peril was threatening him, but that some danger was hanging over my head, the more real in that it was unseen and unsuspected by me.

I called him to me and rewarded him with a caress. He was overjoyed to note that I had apparently understood him. I now made haste to seek out Barrel Brow. He was surprised to feel my salutation. In a moment or so I had told him all. Nor was he slow in detecting my excitement. He, no doubt, felt that in the changed character of my handwriting.

"Calm thyself, little baron," he wrote. "The wise Bulger has told thee the truth. Thy life is in danger. I had resolved to send for thee this very day to warn thee of it: to bid thee quit the land of the Formifolk in all haste, for the notion has spread among our people that it was the dancing spectre at thy heels which caused the death of the gentle Pouting Lip, who disappeared so mysteriously the other day. I therefore counsel thee that thou make ready at once and quit our city to-morrow before the clocks rouse the people from their sleep."

I thanked Barrel Brow, and promised that I would heed his advice, although I confessed to him that I would fain have bided a few weeks longer, there were so many things in and about the wonderful City of Silver that I had not seen. But I owed it to the dear hearts of my own world to take the best care of my life, insignificant though it might appear to me.

Then, again, I felt that it would be madness to attempt to reason with the Soodopsies. To them the dancing spectre at my heels was a real being of flesh and blood, although they had not been able to seize him, and it was really natural for them to suspect that we had made away with Pouting Lip.

Calling out to Bulger to follow me, I left Barrel Brow's home, resolved to make one more round of the wonderful city, and then pack up some food and clothing and be all ready for a start before the clocks began their tapping.

I should explain, dear friends, that, as happens in all cities, the people of this one imagined at times that they hadn't quite elbow room enough, and hence they surveyed other chambers, and set up new candelabra within them, in order to chase the cold and dampness away, and make them fit for human habitations.

In the last one which they had in this way annexed to their fair city, fitting it with a silver doorway and tiling the floor with polished plates of the same beautiful metal, they had discovered a hard mound apparently of rock in one corner, and had resolved that they would come some day with their drills and picks and begin the task of removing this mound.

A strange inclination came upon me to visit this new chamber in order to inspect the work of these eyeless workmen, and see how far they had proceeded with their task of transforming a cold and rocky vault into a bright, warm, healthy habitation.

Imagine my surprise to hear Bulger utter a low growl as we reached the entrance, and I put out my hand to swing the door open, for the Soodopsies were not at work there that day, and the place was as silent as a tomb.

Glancing through the grating, a sight met my gaze which caused my flesh to creep and my hair to stiffen. What think ye was it? Why, the mound in the corner was rocking and swaying, and from underneath one end issued a loud and angry hissing. I'm no coward, if I do say it myself, but this was just a little too much for ordinary or even extraordinary flesh to bear without flinching. I staggered back with a suppressed cry of horror, and was upon the point of breaking into a mad flight, when the thought flashed through my mind that the door was securely fastened, and that there would be no danger in my taking another look at the terrible monster thus caged in this chamber.

A great snake-like head was now lifted from beneath one edge of the mound, on the end of a long, swaying neck. Its great round eyes, big as an ox's, stared with a dull, cold, glassy look from wall to wall, and then, with an awful outburst of hissing, the whole mound was suddenly raised upon four great legs, thick as posts, and ending in terrible claws, and borne rocking and swaying into the centre of the chamber.

What was this terrible monster, and where had it come from?

Why, I saw through it all now at a glance. It was a gigantic tortoise, eight feet long by five wide, at least, and once an inhabitant of the upper world. Thousands and thousands of years ago, by the coming of the awful fields of ice, it had been forced to fly from certain death by crawling down into these underground caverns. Here, chilled and numbed by the dampness and cold, it had fallen asleep, and would have continued to sleep on for other ages to come, had not the industrious Formifolk lighted the clusters of burning jets of gas in the monster's bedroom. Gradually the warmth had penetrated the roof of shell made thicker by earth and layers of broken rock, which the tooth of time had dropped upon it, and reached his great heart, and set it beating again slowly, very slowly, but faster and faster, until he really felt that he had awakened from his long sleep.

By a terrible misfortune, Pouting Lip, the gentle Soodopsy, had happened to be left behind when his brother laborers quit work, and the new silver doors of the chamber had been closed upon him.

Oh, it was terrible to think of, but true it must have been—the poor little Soodopsy, shut in by his own eyeless folk in this chamber, which he was helping to beautify by his patient skill, had served to satisfy the hunger of this awful monster, after his long ages of fasting.

But why, you ask, dear friends, was all this not discovered when the Great Circle had been formed, and the search was made for him? Simply because the monster, after devouring the lost Soodopsy, retreated to his nest and drew the dirt and crumbled rock up around him with his gigantic flippers, and went to sleep again, as all gorged reptiles do, so that when the searchers entered the new chamber all was as they had left it, the mound of rock, as they had supposed it to be, in the corner undisturbed.

With Bulger at my heels I now turned and ran with such mad haste to Barrel Brow's, that the whole city was thrown into the wildest disorder, for, of course, they had felt me fly past them.

With all the quickness I could command, I wrote an account of what I had witnessed, and when Barrel Brow communicated it to the assembled Soodopsies, a thousand hands flew into the air, in token of mingled fright and wonder, and a wild rush was made for Bulger and me, and we were well-nigh smothered with kisses and caresses.

The moment the excitement had quieted down a little, a Great Circle was immediately formed, and I was honored with a place in it, and when my tablet was passed about, a thousand hands made signs of assent.

My plan was a simple one: it was to make a pipe connection between Uphaslok and the new chamber, and to turn the deadly vapor into the sleeping apartment of the gigantic monster. In this manner his despatch would be a happy one, merely a beginning of another one of his long naps, so far as he would know any thing about it.

This was done at once, care first being taken to make the doors of the new chamber perfectly air tight. I was the first to enter the cavern after the execution of the monster, and found, to my delight, that my estimate of his length and width was correct almost to an inch.

I always had a wonderful eye for dimension and distances.

Seeing Bulger raising himself upon his hind legs, and make an effort to dislodge something from the wall, I drew near to assist him.

Alas! it was dear, gentle, Pouting Lip's tablet. He had been writing upon it, and as the terrible monster advanced upon him, he had reached up and hung it upon a silver pin on the wall. When the Soodopsies read what their poor brother had written, there they all sat down and wrung their hands in silent but awful grief: it ran as follows:—

"O my people! why have ye abandoned me? The air trembles; the whole place is filled with suffocating odor. Must I die? Alas, I fear it! and yet I would so love to feel my dear ones' touches once more! The ground trembles; a stifling breath is puffed into my face; I am wearied, almost fainting, by trying to escape it. I can write no more. Don't grieve too long over me. It was my fault. I stayed behind, when I should have followed. Oh, horrible, horrible! Farewell! I'm going now. A loving touch to all—farewell!"

After waiting a few days for the grief of the Formifolk to lighten a little, I asked them to send a number of their most skilful workmen to assist me in removing the magnificent shell from the dead monster whose body was fed to the fishes. They not only did this, but they also offered to transform the shell into a beautiful boat for me, so that when I resolved to bid them adieu, I might sail away from the City of Silver and not be obliged to trudge along the Marble Highway. The work went on apace. At first the polishers began their task, and in a few days the mighty carapace glowed like a lady's comb. Then the dainty and cunning craftsmen in silver began their part of the work, and ere many days the shell was fitted with a silver prow curiously wrought, like a swan's neck and head, while quaintly carved trimmings ran here and there, and a dainty pair of silver sculls with a silver rudder, beautifully chased, from which ran two little silken ropes, were added to the outfit. I never had seen anything half so rich and rare, and I was as proud of it as a young king of his throne before he finds it is so much like my ship of shell.

At last the day came when I was to bid the gentle Soodopsies a long farewell.

They lined the shore as Bulger and I proceeded to take our place in the bark of shell which sat upon the water like a thing of life.

It was with a great show of dignity that Bulger took his position in the stern with the tiller-ropes in his mouth, ready to pull on either side as I might direct; and setting the silver oars in place, I threw my weight upon them, and away we glided, swiftly and noiselessly, over the surface of the dark and sluggish stream.

In a few moments nothing but a faint glimmer was left to remind us of the wonderful City of Silver, where the silent Formifolk live and love and labor without ever a thought that human beings could be any happier than they. Dear, happy folk, they have solved a mighty problem which we of the upper world are still struggling over.

CHAPTER XXI

HOW WE WERE LIGHTED ON OUR WAY DOWN THE DARK AND SILENT RIVER.—SUDDEN AND FIERCE ONSLAUGHT UPON OUR BEAUTIFUL BOAT OF SHELL.—A FIGHT FOR LIFE AGAINST TERRIBLE ODDS, AND HOW BULGER STOOD BY ME THROUGH IT ALL.—COLD AIR AND LUMPS OF ICE.—OUR ENTRY INTO THE CAVERN WHENCE THEY CAME.—THE BOAT OF SHELL COMES TO THE END OF ITS VOYAGE.—SUNLIGHT IN THE WORLD WITHIN A WORLD, AND ALL ABOUT THE WONDERFUL WINDOW THROUGH WHICH IT POURED, AND THE MYSTERIOUS LAND IT LIGHTED.

I dare say, dear friends, that you are puzzling your brains to think out how it was possible for me to row away from the wonderful city of the Formifolk without running our boat continually ashore. Ah, you forget that the keen-eyed Bulger was at the helm, and that it was not the first time that he had piloted me through darkness impenetrable to my eyes; but more than this: I soon discovered that the plashing of my silver oars kept my little friends, the fire lizards, in a constant state of alarm, and although I couldn't hear the crackling of their tails, yet the tiny flashes of light served to outline the shore admirably. So I pulled away with a will, and down this dark and silent river, for there was a current, although hardly perceptible,

Bulger and I were borne along in the beautiful bark of tortoise shell with its prow of carved and burnished silver.

During my sojourn in the Land of the Soodopsies I had one day, while calling upon the learned Barrel Brow, noticed a beautifully carved silver hand-lamp of the Pompeian pattern among his curiosities. I asked him if he knew what it was. He replied that he did, adding that it had doubtless been brought from the upper world by his people, and he begged me to accept it as a keepsake. I did so, and upon leaving the City of Silver, I filled it with fish-oil and fitted a silken wick to it. It was well that I had done so, for after a while the fire lizards disappeared entirely, and Bulger and I would have been left in total darkness, had I not drawn forth my beautiful silver lamp, lighted it, and suspended it from the beak of the silver swan which curved its graceful neck above the bow of our boat.

After lying on my oars long enough to set some food before Bulger and partake of some myself, I again started on my voyage down the silent river, no longer shrouded in impenetrable gloom.

I had not taken over half a dozen strokes, when suddenly one of my oars was almost twisted out of my hand by a vicious tug, from some inhabitant of these dark and sluggish waters. I resolved to quicken my stroke in order to escape another such a wrench, for the silver oars fashioned by the Soodopsies for me were of very delicate make, intended only for very gentle usage. Suddenly another vicious snap was made at my other oar; and this time the animal succeeded in retaining its hold, for I dared not attempt to wrench the oar out of its grip, for fear of breaking it. It was a large crustacean of the crab family, and its milk-white shell gave it a ghost-like look as it struggled about in the black waters, fiercely intent to keep its hold upon the oar. The next instant a similar creature had fastened firmly upon my other oar, and there I sat utterly helpless. But worse than this, the dark waters were now fairly alive with these white armored guards of this underworld stream, each apparently bent upon setting an immediate end to my progress through their domain. They now began a series of furious efforts to lay hold of the sides of my boat with their huge claws, but happily its polished surface made this impossible for them to accomplish.

Up to this moment Bulger had not stirred a muscle or uttered a sound, but now a sharp growl from him told me that something serious had happened at his end of the boat. It was serious indeed, for several of the largest of the fierce crustaceans had laid hold of the rudder and were wrenching it from side to side as if to tear it off. Every attempt of course caused a tug at the tiller-ropes held between Bulger's teeth; but, bracing himself firmly, he resisted their furious efforts as well as he could, and succeeded in saving the rudder for the time being.

All of a sudden our frail bark of shell crashed into some sort of obstruction, and came to a dead standstill. Peering into the darkness, to my horror I saw that the wily enemy had spanned the river with chains made up of living links by each laying hold of his neighbor's claw, the chain thus formed being then rendered almost as strong as steel by the interweaving of their double rows of small hooked legs.

Our advance was not only blocked, but death, an awful death, seemed to be staring us in the face; for what possible hope of escape could there be if Bulger and I should leap into the water, now alive with these fast swimming creatures, whirling their huge claws about in search for some way to get at us. From the brave manner in which Bulger was holding the madly swinging helm, I saw that he was determined not to surrender. But alas, bravery is but a sorry thing for two to fight a thousand with! And yet I had not lost my head—don't think that.

True, I was hard pressed; the very dust of the balance, if thicker on their side, might make my scale kick the beam.

I had hauled both oars into the boat by reaching over and beating off the claws fastened upon them, and had up to this moment driven back every one of the fierce creatures which had succeeded in throwing one of his claws over the edge of the boat; but now, to my horror, I felt that our little craft was being slowly but surely drawn stern first toward the river bank. In order to accomplish this, the crustaceans had thrown out a line composed of their bodies gripped together, and had made it fast to the rudder. Not an instant was to be lost!

Once upon the river bank, the fierce creatures would swarm around us by the tens of thousands, drag us down, pinch us to death, and tear us piecemeal!

SAILING AWAY FROM THE LAND OF THE SOODOPSIES.

An idea flashed upon me—it was this: it is folly to attempt to resist these countless swarms of crustaceans by the use of one pair of weak hands, even though they be aided by Bulger's keen and willing teeth. We should, after a brief struggle, go down as the brave man in the sewer went down, when the famished rats leaped upon him from every side at once, or as the stray buffalo goes down when the pack of ravenous wolves closes up its circle about him. If I am to save my life, it must be by striking a blow that will reach every one of these small but fierce enemies at the same instant, and thus paralyze them, or, at least, bewilder them, until I can succeed in making my escape!

Quickly drawing my brace of pistols, I held their muzzles close to the water, and discharged them at the same instant. The effect was terrific. Like a crash of a terrible thunderbolt, the report burst forth and echoed through these vast and silent chambers, until it seemed as if the great vaulted roof of rock had by some awful convulsion of nature been cast roaring and rattling down upon the face of these black and sluggish waters! When the smoke had cleared away, a strange but welcome sight met my gaze. Tens of thousands of the huge crabs floated lifeless upon the surface of the river, with their shells split by the concussion the full length of their bodies.

It proved to have been a masterly stroke on my part, and, dear friends, you will believe me when I tell you that I drew a deep breath as I set my silver oars against the thole-pins, and, having worked my boat clear of the swarms of stunned crustaceans, rowed away for dear life!

Dear life! Ah, yes, dear life, for whose life is not dear to him, even though it be dark and gloomy at times? Is there not always something, or some one, to live for? Is there not always a glimmer of hope that the morrow's sun will go up brighter than it did this morning? Well, anyway, I repeat that I rowed away for dear life, while Bulger held the tiller-ropes and kept our frail bark of polished shell in the middle of the stream.

Whether the air was actually colder, or whether it was merely the natural chill that so often strikes the human heart after it has been beating and throbbing with alternate hope and fear, I couldn't say at the time; but I knew this much, that I suddenly found myself suffering from the cold.

For the first time since my descent into the World within a World, the air nipped my finger-tips; that soft, balmy, June-like atmosphere was gone, and I made haste to put on my fur-trimmed top-coat, which I had not made much use of lately.

At that moment one of my oars struck against some hard substance floating in the waters. I put out my hand to feel of it. To my great surprise it proved to be a lump of ice, and very soon another and another went floating by us.

We were most surely entering a region where it was cold enough to make ice. I was not sorry for this; for, to tell the truth, Bulger and I were both beginning to feel the effects of our long sojourn in the rocky chambers of this under world, whose atmosphere, though soft and warm, yet lacked the elasticity of the open air.

Ice caverns would be a complete change, and the cold air would, no doubt, send our blood tingling through our veins just as if we were out a-sleighing in the upper world on a winter's night, when the stars twinkle over our heads and the snow crystals creak beneath our runners.

Soon now huge icicles began to dot the roof of rock that spanned the river, and shafts and columns of ice dimly visible along the shore seemed to be standing there like silent sentries, watching our boat as it threaded its way through the ever-narrowing channel. And now, too, a faint glow of light reached us from I knew not where, so that by straining my eyes I could see that the river had taken a sweep, and entered a vast cavern with roof and walls of ice fretted and carved into fantastic depths and niches and shelves and cornices, with here and there shapes so fanciful that it seemed to me I had entered some vast hall of statuary, where hero and warrior, nymph and maiden, shepherd and bird-catcher, filled these shelves and niches in glorious array. Farther advance by water was impossible, for the blocks of ice, knitted together like a floe, closed the river completely. I therefore determined to make a landing—draw my boat upon the shore, and continue my journey on foot.

The mysterious light which up to this moment had shed its pale glimmer like an arctic night upon the roofs and walls of ice of these silent chambers now began to strengthen so that Bulger and I had no difficulty in picking our way along the shore. In fact, we crossed and recrossed the river itself when the whim seized us, for it now went winding on ahead of us, like a broad ribbon of ice through caverns and corridors.

Suddenly I came to a halt and stood as motionless as the fantastic forms of ice surrounding me. What could it mean? Were my eyes weakened by my long sojourn in the World within a World, playing me cruel tricks? Surely there can be no mistake! I whispered to myself. That light yonder which pours its glorious effulgence upon those spires and pinnacles, those towers and turrets of ice, is the sunshine of the upper world! Can it be that my marvellous underground journey is ended, that I stand upon the threshold of the upper world once more?

Bulger, too, recognizes this flood of sunshine, and breaking out into a fit of joyous barking, dashes on ahead, to be the first one to feel its gentle warmth after our long journey through the dark and silent passages of the World within a World.

But I dare not trust my eyes, and fearing lest he should fall into some ambush or meet with some dread accident, I called him back to me.

Together we hurry along as rapidly as possible. Now I note that we are drawing near to the end of the vast corridor through which we have been making our way for some time, and that we stand upon the portal of a mighty subterranean region lighted with real sunlight. It stretches away as far as the eye can reach, and so high is the roof that spans this vast under world that I cannot see whether it be of ice or not. All that I can see is that through one of its sloping sides there streams a mighty torrent of sunlight, which pours its splendor with unstinting hand upon the wide highways, the broad terraces, the sheer parapets, and the sloping banks which diversify this ice world. Can it be that one side of this mighty mountain which nature has here hollowed out and set like a peaked roof over this vast subterranean region, is a gigantic window of ice itself through which the sunlight of the outer world streams in this grand way like a silent cataract of light, like a deluge of sunshine? No, this could not be; for now upon a second look I saw that this flood of light thus streaming through the side of the mountain came through it like a mighty pencil of rays, and striking the opposite walls with its brilliancy a hundred-fold increased, rebounded in a thousand directions, flooding the whole region with its effulgence and dying away in faint and pearl-like glimmer in the vast approach where I had first noted it.

And therefore I understood that nature must have set a gigantic lens, twice a thousand feet or more in diameter, in the sloping side of this hollow mountain—a perfect lens of purest rock crystal, which, gathering in its mysterious bosom the sunlight of the outer world, threw it—intensely radiant and dazzling white—into the gloomy depths of this World within a World, so that when the sun went up out there, it went up in here as well, but became cold as it was beautiful, bringing no warmth, no other cheer save light, to this subterranean region which for thousands of centuries had lain locked in the crystal embrace of frozen lakes and brooks and rivers and torrents and waterfalls, once bubbling and flowing and rushing headlong through fair lands of the upper world, but suddenly checked in their course by some bursting forth of mighty pent-up forces, and turned downward into these icy depths condemned to everlasting rest and silence, their crystals locked in a sleep that never would know an awaking, mocked in their dreams by this mysterious sunlight that came with the smile and the fair, winsome look of the real, and yet was so powerless to set them free as once it did when the springtime came in the upper world. All these thoughts and many others besides flitted through my mind as I stood looking up at that mighty lens in its setting of mightier rock.

And so deeply impressed was I by the sight of such a great flood of sunlight pouring through this gigantic bull's eye which nature had set in the rocky side of the hollow mountain peak and illumining this under world, that the longer I gazed upon the wonderful spectacle the more firmly inthralled my senses became by it.

The deep silence, the deliciously pure air, the ever-varying tints of the light as the mighty ice columns acting the part of prisms, literally filled those vast chambers with the rainbow's glorious glow, imparted unto the spell resting upon me such unearthly power that it might have held me there until my limbs hardened into icy crystals and my eyes looked out with a frozen stare, had not the ever-watchful Bulger given a gentle tug at the skirt of my coat and aroused me from my inthralling meditation.

CHAPTER XXII

THE PALACE OF ICE IN THE GOLDEN SUNLIGHT, AND WHAT I IMAGINED IT MIGHT CONTAIN.—HOW WE WERE HALTED BY A COUPLE OF QUAINTLY CLAD SENTINELS.—THE KOLTYKWERPS.—HIS FRIGID MAJESTY KING GELIDUS.—MORE ABOUT THE ICE PALACE, TOGETHER WITH A DESCRIPTION OF THE THRONE-ROOM.—OUR RECEPTION BY THE KING AND HIS DAUGHTER SCHNEEBOULE.—BRIEF MENTION OF BULLIBRAIN, OR LORD HOT HEAD.

Scarcely had I advanced a hundred yards beyond the portal where I had halted when happening to turn my eyes to the other side, a sight met them which sent a thrill of wonder and delight through my form. There upon the highest terrace stood a palace of ice, its slender minarets, its high-lifted towers, its rounded turrets, its spacious platform, and its broad flights of steps all glittering in the sunlight as if gem-studded and jewel-set.

It was a spectacle to stir the most indifferent heart, let alone one so full of ardor and buoyancy as mine. But ah, dear friends, even admitting that I can succeed in awakening in your minds even a faint conception of the beauty of this ice palace, as the sunlight fell full upon it at that moment, how can I ever hope to give you an idea of the unearthly beauty of this palace of ice and its glorious surroundings when the moon went up in the outer world at a later hour and its pale, mysterious light was poured through the mighty lens in the mountain side, and fell with celestial shimmer upon these walls of ice?

But the one thought that oppressed me now was: Can this beautiful abode be without a tenant, without a living soul within its wonderful halls and chambers? Or, may not its dwellers, overtaken by the pitiless cold, sit with wide-opened eyes and icy glare, stark as marble in chairs of ice, white frosted hair pressed against icy cushions, and hands stiffened around crystal cups filled with frozen wine of topaz hue, while the harper's fingers cling cramped to the wires stiff as the wires themselves, and the last tones of the singer's voice lie in feathery crystals of frozen breath white at his feet?

Come what may, I resolved to lift the crystal knocker that might hang on the outer door of this palace of ice and awaken the castellan, if his slumber were not that of death. In a few moments I had crossed the level space between me and the first terrace, which it would be necessary for me to scale in order to reach the second and then the third upon which stood the palace of ice.

Imagine my more than surprise upon finding myself now at the foot of a magnificent flight of steps, hewn into the ice with a master hand, and leading to the terrace above.

Springing lightly up this flight with Bulger close at my heels, I suddenly set eyes upon two of the quaintest-looking human beings that I ever remembered seeing in all my travels. They looked for all the world like two big animated snowballs, being clad from top to toe in garments made of snow-white fleece, their skull-caps likewise of white fur, leaving only their faces visible. In his right hand each of them carried a very prettily shaped flint axe, mounted upon a helve of polished bone.

Striding up to me and swinging their axes over my head in altogether too close proximity to my poll to be particularly pleasant, one of them cries out,—

"Halt, sir! Unless his frigid Majesty Gelidus, King of the Koltykwerps, awaits thy coming, his guards will, at a signal from us, roll a few thousand tons of ice down upon thee if thou darest proceed another step. Therefore, stand fast and tell us who thou art and whether thou art expected."

"Gentlemen," said I, "kindly lower those axes of yours and I will convince you that his frigid Majesty hath nothing to dread in me, for I am none other than the very small but very noble and very famous Sebastian von Troomp, commonly known as 'Little Baron Trump.'"

"Never heard of thee in all my life," said both of the guards as with one voice.

"But I have of you, gentlemen," I continued,—for now I recollected what the learned Don Fum had said about the frozen land of the Koltykwerps, or Cold Bodies,—"and as proof of my peaceful intent, like a true knight I now offer you my hand, and beg that you will conduct me into the presence of his frigid Majesty."

No sooner had the guard standing next me drawn off his glove and grasped my hand, than he let it loose again with a cry of fright.

"Zounds! Man, art thou on fire? Why, thy hand burned me like the flame of a lamp!"

"Why, no, my friend," said I quietly; "that's my ordinary temperature."

"And thy companion?"

"Hath even a warmer heart than I have," was my reply.

"Well, our word for it, little baron," exclaimed one of the guards with a chuckle, "there will be no place for thee except in the meat quarry. Possibly after thou hast been cooled off for a week or so, his frigid Majesty will be able to have thee about!"

This was not a very cheerful prospect, for I had no particular desire to be laid away in the royal ice-box for a week or so. Anyway, the only thing to be done was to insist upon being conducted at once into the presence of the King of the Koltykwerps, and abide by his decision.

One of the guards having saluted me by presenting his battle-axe in real military style, faced about and began to ascend the grand staircase with intent to announce my arrival to his frigid Majesty, while the other informed me that he would conduct me as far as the perron of the palace.

I was wonderstruck with the beauty of the three staircases leading up to the ice palace. Massive balustrades with curiously carved balusters springing from towering pedestals, crowned with beautiful lamps, all, all, I say, all and everything, to the crystal-clear sides of the lamps themselves, was fashioned from blocks of ice. It proved to be a good climb to the top of the third terrace, and I was not put out when the guard solemnly lowered his battle-axe of flint to bring me to a standstill.

The sun in the upper world was, no doubt, nearing the horizon, for a deep and beautiful twilight suddenly sank upon the icy dominions of King Gelidus, and, to my surprise and delight, through the great slabs of crystal-clear ice which served for windows to the palace, streamed a soft radiance as if a thousand wax tapers were burning in the chambers and galleries in-doors. It was a sight to gladden the eyes of any mortal; but if I had been spellbound by the beauty of its exterior, how shall I tell you, dear friends, of the curious splendor of the interior of Gelidus' palace of ice, as it burst upon me when I had crossed its threshold?

Hallway led into hallway, chamber opened into chamber, through portals gracefully arched, and winding staircases climbed to upper rooms, while hanging from lofty ceilings or resting on graceful pedestals, were a thousand alabaster lamps, shedding light and perfume upon this glorious home of his frigid Majesty Gelidus, King of the Koltykwerps. Long rows of retainers, all in snow-white fur, lined the wide hallway, as the guards conducted Bulger and me into the palace and bowed in silence as we passed.

To my more than wonder, I saw that the inner rooms were most sumptuously furnished, chairs and divans being scattered here and there, all covered with superb skins of white fur, while the floor, too, was carpeted with them, and as the soft radiance of the alabaster lamps fell upon these magnificent pelts and set ten thousand jewels in the walls and ceilings of ice, I was ready to admit that I had never seen anything half so beautiful. And yet I was still outside the throne-room of his frigid Majesty!

At length we came to one end of a broad hallway which seemed shut off from the rest of the palace by a wall thickly incrusted with strings of great diamonds, each as big as a goose-egg, extending from the ceiling to the floor, and turning back the shimmer of the lamps with such a flood of crystalline radiance that my eyes involuntarily closed before it.

Think of my amazement when the two guards, laying hold of this wall of jewels, as I deemed it, drew it to the right and left till there was room for me to pass. What I had taken for a wall of jewels was but a curtain made up of round bits of ice strung upon strings and hanging like a shower of diamonds there before me, as they glittered in the light of the lamps each side of them.

I now stood in the throne-room of his frigid Majesty, the King of the Koltykwerps. Now I realized that what I had seen elsewhere in his palace of ice was in reality but a sample of its magnificence, for here the splendor of King Gelidus' castle burst upon me in its fullest strength. Imagine a great round chamber lighted with the soft flames of perfumed oil, streaming from a hundred alabaster lamps, the walls lined with broad divans covered with snow-white pelts, the floors thickly carpeted with the same glorious rugs, while on one side, glittering in the shimmer of the hundred massive lamps, stands the icy throne of the King of the Koltykwerps, decked with snow-white skins, and he upon it, with Schneeboule, his fair daughter, sitting at his feet, and all around and about him, group-wise, a hundred Koltykwerps, the king, the princess, and the courtiers all clad in skins whiter than the driven snow, and you, dear friends, will have some faint idea of the splendor of the scene which burst upon me as the two guards drew aside the strands of ice jewels at the end of the hallway in the palace of ice!

Like all his subjects, King Gelidus looked out through the round window of his fur hood, just as a big good-natured boy does through his skating-cap.

THE BATTLE FOR LIFE WITH THE WHITE CRABS.

The Koltykwerps were not much taller than I, but were very stocky built, so that when broadened out by their thick fur suits they really took on at times the appearance of animated snowballs. It would be hard for the fingers of the deftest hand to draw faces fuller of kindliness and good nature than those of the Koltykwerps. Their small, honest gray eyes sparkled with a boniform glint, and so broad were their smiles that they were only about half visible through the round holes of their fur hoods. I was delighted with them from the very start, and the more so when I heard King Gelidus cry out in a cheery voice: "A right crisp and cold welcome to our icy court, little baron; but from what our people tell us, thou carriest a pair of hands so hot that we beg thee to take a few days to cool off before thou touchest palms with any of the Koltykwerps, and we also beg thee to be careful and not to lean against any of our richly carved panels, or to slide down any of our highly polished railings, or to handle the strands of our jewels, or sit down for any length of time on the front steps of our palace. And we make the same request of thy four-footed companion, who is said to be of even a warmer disposition than thou."

I bowed and kissed my hand to his frigid Majesty, and assured him that I should make every effort to lower my temperature as speedily as possible, and, in the mean time, that I should be extremely careful not to come into contact with any of the artistic carving of his palace of ice.

As I pronounced these words, the whole company began to clap their hands; and as they did so, a cold shiver ran down my back, for there was a sound, methought, very much like the rattling of dry bones to that applause, but I took good care not to let King Gelidus notice my fright.

His frigid Majesty now presented me to his daughter Schneeboule, a pretty little maid of about sixteen crystal winters, with cheeks round as apples, and as deeply dimpled as the furrows of a cross-bun. Her eyes twinkled as she looked upon Bulger and me, and turning to her frigid papa, she asked for leave to touch the tip end of my thumb, which being done, she gave a squeaky little scream and began to blow on her tiny finger as if I had blistered it.

King Gelidus also presented me to several of his court favorites, all men of the coldest blood in the nation. Their names were Jellikin, Phrostyphiz, Icikul, and Glacierbhoy. They were all dreadfully slow thinkers when you questioned them very closely upon any subject.

It didn't take me very long to discover this. In fact, they requested me to be less warm in my manner, and not to ask them any posers, as they invariably found that deep thought caused a rise in their temperature.

This was, to be honest about it, very annoying to me; for you know, dear friends, what a loadstone my mind is, never asleep, always in a quiver like a mariner's compass, pointing this way and that, in search of the polar star of wisdom.

Upon making known my trouble to his frigid Majesty, King Gelidus, he most gracefully ordered one of his trusty attendants to conduct me to the triple walled ice-cell of a certain Koltykwerp by the name of Bullibrain, that is, literally, "Boiling Brain," a man who had been born with a hot head, and consequently with a very active brain. For fifty years King Gelidus had been doing his very best to refrigerate this subject of his, but without success. As I was just bursting with impatience to ask a whole string of questions concerning the Koltykwerps, you may imagine how delighted I was to make the acquaintance of Bullibrain, or Lord Hot Head as he was called among the

Koltykwerps; but, dear friends, you must excuse me if I make this the end of a chapter and stop here for a brief rest.

CHAPTER XXIII

LORD HOT HEAD AGAIN, AND, THIS TIME A FULLER ACCOUNT OF HIM.—HIS WONDROUS TALES CONCERNING THE KOLTYKWERPS: WHERE THEY CAME FROM, WHO THEY WERE, AND HOW THEY MANAGED TO LIVE IN THIS WORLD OF ETERNAL FROST.—THE MANY QUESTIONS I PUT TO HIM, AND HIS ANSWERS IN FULL.

Lord Bullibrain was never allowed to set foot inside the palace of ice. King Gelidus, backed by the opinion of his favorites, still indulged the belief that he would be able in the end to refrigerate him. True, he had been many years at the task, so that it had now become a sort of hobby of his, and almost daily did his frigid Majesty pay a visit to his hot-headed subject and test his temperature by pressing a small ball of ice against his temples. To King Gelidus' mind, a man of so high a temperature was a continual menace to the peace and quiet of his kingdom. What if Lord Hot Head in a dream should wander forth some night and fall asleep with his back against one of the walls of the ice palace? Might he not melt away enough of it to throw the whole glorious fabric into a slump and slush of débris? It was terrible to think of, when he did think of it, and he thought of it quite often.

But Bullibrain had no terrors for me, nor for Bulger either; in fact, Bulger was delighted to be stroked by a warm hand, and he and Bullibrain and I soon became the very best of friends; but his frigid Majesty was so alarmed when he heard of this friendship, that he was seized with quite a spasm of warmth, for, thought he, the united heat of three hot heads might work some terrible harm to the welfare of his people. So he issued the coldest kind of a decree carved on a tablet of ice, that Bullibrain and I should on no one day pass more than a half-hour together; that we should never touch palm to palm, sleep in the same room, eat from the same dish, or sit on the same divan.

These regulations were annoying, but I followed them to the letter; and when King Gelidus saw how careful I was to yield the strictest obedience to his decree, he conceived a genuine affection for me and sent several magnificent pelts to the ice-house, which had been assigned to Bulger and me, for, of course, it would not have been safe for us to lodge in the palace itself, but his frigid Majesty held out the flattering prospect that the very moment Bulger and I should become properly refrigerated, apartments in the palace would be assigned to us, and, in fact, that I should be permitted to eat at the royal table.

Who are the Koltykwerps? Where did these strange folk come from? How did they ever find their way down into this World of Eternal Frost? And, above all, where do they get their food and clothing from? These were a few of the questions which I was so impatient to have answered that my temperature was raised a whole degree, and I was obliged to sleep with only one single pelt between me and my divan of crystal ice.

For a man bred and born in so cold a country as the land of the Koltykwerps, Bullibrain had an extremely quick and active mind. On account of his rapid heart-beat, and the consequent high temperature of his body, he was not able to do his writing on slabs of ice as other learned Koltykwerps had done, for it would not have been a pleasant thing for him to see a poem which he had just finished literally melt away in his hands, without so much as leaving an ink-stain behind, so he had been obliged, with King Gelidus' permission, to do his writing on thin tablets of alabaster.

Before he began to talk to me about the progenitors of the Koltykwerps, he showed me a map of the country in the upper world once inhabited by them, and traced for me the course they had sailed upon abandoning that country, and described the beautiful shores they had landed upon in their search for a new home. I saw at a glance that it was Greenland which Bullibrain was thus unconsciously describing; and knowing as I did that in past ages Greenland had been a land of blue skies, warm winds, green meadows, and fertile valleys, before moving mountains of ice came down from the North and crushed all life out of it, I listened with breathless interest to his wonderful tales of its beautiful lakes, nestled at the foot of vine-clad mountains, all of which Bullibrain now looked upon in fair visions inherited from his ancestors. And I also knew that it must have been the Arctic Ocean which had been traversed by the ships of the Koltykwerps, who had then landed upon the, in those days, sunny shores of Northern Russia.

But the mountains of ice could sail too, and they followed the fleeing Koltykwerps like mighty monsters, dashing themselves with terrible roar and crash upon the peaceful shores, which they soon transformed into a wilderness of berg, of glacier, and of floe.

Only a handful of the Koltykwerps survived; and these, in their dumb despair taking refuge in the clefts and caverns of the North Urals, could from their hiding-places look upon one of the strangest sights that had ever greeted human eyes. So rapid had been the advance of these mighty masses of ice, crashing against the mountain sides and rending the very rocks in their fury, that the air gave up its warmth, and the sun was powerless to give it back again. The animals of the wild wood and the beasts of the field, overtaken in their flight, perished as they ran and stood there stark and stiff, with heads uptossed and muscles knotted. Them by the thousands and ten times thousands the crushed crystals of the pursuing floods caught up like moss and leaves in a mountain torrent and packed in every cave and cavern on the way, tearing broader and loftier portals into these subterranean chambers, so that they might do their work the better!

"And these, then, O Bullibrain, are your meat quarries," I exclaimed, "whence ye draw your daily food?"

"Even so, little baron," replied the hot-headed Koltykwerp, "and not only our food, but the skins which serve us so admirably for clothing in this cold, under ground world, and the oil, too, which burns in our beautiful alabaster lamps, besides a hundred other things, such as bone for helves and handles, horn for needles and buttons and eating utensils, wool for the weaving of our undergarments, and magnificent pelts of bear and seal and walrus, which, laid upon our benches and divans of crystal ice, transform them into beds and couches which even an inhabitant of thy world might envy."

"But, O Bullibrain," I cried out, "have ye not almost exhausted these supplies? Will not death from starvation soon stare ye all in the face in these deep and icy caverns of the under world, visited by the sun's light yet unwarmed by it?"

"Nay, little baron," answered Bullibrain with a smile almost as warm as one of my own; "let not that thought give thee a moment's alarm, for we have as yet barely raised the lid of this ice-box of nature's packing. We are not large eaters any way," continued Lord Hot Head, "for while it is true that we are not indolent people, for his frigid Majesty's palace and our dwellings need constant repair, and new hatchets and axes must be chipped out in the flint quarries and new lamps carved and new garments woven, yet it is also true that we take life rather easy. We have no enemies to slay, no quarrels to settle, no gold to fight over, no land to drive our fellow-creatures from and fence in; nor can we be ill, if we were willing to be, for in this pure, cold, crisp air disease would try in vain to sow her poison germs; hence, needing no doctors, we have none, as we have no lawyers either, or merchants to sell us what belongs to us already. His frigid Majesty is an excellent king. I never read of a better one. I doubt that his like exists in the upper world. Always cool headed, no thought of conquest, no dreams of power, no longings for empty pomp and show ever enter his mind. Since the day his father died and we set the great Koltykwerp crown of crystal ice upon his cool brow, his temperature has never risen but a half a degree, and that was only for a brief hour or so, and was occasioned by a mad proposal of one of his councillors, who claimed that he had discovered an explosive compound, something like the gunpowder of thy world, I fancy, by which he could shatter the glorious window of rock crystal set in the mountain dome of our under world and let in the warm sunshine."

"Did his frigid Majesty Gelidus put this daring Koltykwerp to death?" I asked.

"Oh, dear, no," replied Bullibrain; "he merely ordered him to be refrigerated for so many hours a day until all his feverish projects had been chilled to death; for no doubt, little baron, a man of thy deep learning knows full well that all the ills which thy world suffers from are the children of fevered brains, of minds made restless and visionary by the high temperature of the blood which gallops through the approaches to the dome of thought, stirring up wild dreams and visions as thy sun lifts the poisonous vapor from the stagnant pool."

The more I listened to Bullibrain the more I liked him. The fact of the matter is, I preferred to sit in his narrow cell with its plain walls of ice lighted up by a single alabaster lamp and converse with him to loitering in the splendid throne-room of his frigid Majesty King Gelidus; but Bulger had discovered that the pelts of Princess Schneeboule's divan were much thicker, softer, and warmer than the single one allowed Lord Hot Head, and therefore he preferred spending his time with her; but fearing lest he might get into mischief, I didn't dare to leave him alone with the princess too long at a time.

CHAPTER XXIV

SOME FEW THINGS CONCERNING THE DEAR LITTLE PRINCESS SCHNEEBOULE.—HOW SHE AND I BECAME FAST FRIENDS, AND HOW ONE DAY SHE CONDUCTED BULGER AND ME INTO HER FAVORITE GROTTO TO SEE THE LITTLE MAN WITH THE FROZEN SMILE.—SOMETHING ABOUT HIM.—WHAT CAME OF MY HAVING LOOKED UPON HIM QUITE FULLY DESCRIBED.

At the time of Bulger's and my arrival in the land of the Koltykwerps the Princess Schneeboule was about fifteen years of age, and I must say that rarely had it been my good fortune to make the acquaintance of such a sweet-tempered, lovable little creature. She flitted about the ice palace like a beam of sunlight, and there was nothing of the spoiled child about her, although a bit mischievous at times.

Her voice was as full of music as a skylark's, and it was not many days before she and I had become the best friends in the world.

Now, you must know, dear friends, that according to the law of the Koltykwerps, a princess is left absolutely free to choose her own husband, and his frigid Majesty was very anxious that Schneeboule should pick hers out as soon as possible. Moreover, the law of the land gave her perfect freedom to choose a husband of high or low degree, provided he was young enough. The way in which a

Koltykwerp princess was required to make known her preference was to press a kiss upon the cheek of the young man whom she might settle upon. This ennobled him at once, and he became the heir apparent to the throne of ice, and entitled to sit on its steps until he should be crowned king.

Now, his frigid Majesty was delighted to see this friendship spring up between Schneeboule and me, for he hoped to make use of my influence to bring her to set the necessary kiss on some youth's cheek before I took my departure from the cold Kingdom of the Koltykwerps. I gave him the word of a nobleman that I would do my best to carry out his wishes.

With Schneeboule for a guide, Bulger and I often went for walks through the splendid ice grottos of her father's kingdom, selecting days when the sunlight of the outer world poured strongest through the mighty lens set in the side of the mountain. Then these grottos took on a splendor that my poor tongue is powerless to describe. Their crystal mazes glittered as if their walls were set with massive jewels most wonderfully cut and polished, and as if their ceilings were fretted with gems so peerless that all the gold of the upper world would fall far short of paying for them. Here, there, and everywhere the skill of the Koltykwerps had carved and chiselled graceful flights of steps, broad landings with majestic columns, and winding corridors lined with long rows of statues, single and groupwise; and ever and anon the visitor came upon a terrace where, seated upon a fur-covered divan, he might look out upon the bewildering beauty of King Gelidus' icy domains, arch touching arch and dome springing from dome, while over and above all, through the gigantic lens in its granite setting, a mile above our heads, streamed a flood of glorious sunlight, lighting up this World within a World with a radiance so grand and so complete as to seem to be a sun of a far greater splendor than the one that warmed the upper world and bathed it in so many gorgeous hues at morn and eve. Hardly a day went by now that the princess of the Koltykwerps did not surprise either Bulger or me with some gift or other.

To tell the truth, dear friends, although my Russian coat was fur-trimmed, yet I began to feel the need of warmer garments after a week's sojourn in the icy domain of King Gelidus, and I think Schneeboule must have heard my teeth chattering, for one morning, upon entering the Palace of Ice, I was delighted to be presented with a full suit of fur precisely similar to the one worn by King Gelidus himself.

Nor was Bulger forgotten by the loving little Princess, for with her own hands she had knitted him a blanket of the softest wool, which she belted so snugly around his body and tied so tightly around his neck that henceforth he felt perfectly comfortable in the chill air of the home of the Koltykwerps.

One day the Princess Schneeboule said to me,—

"Oh, come, little baron, come to my favorite grotto, now that the sun's rays are bright within it; there shalt thou see a wonder."

"A wonder, Princess Schneeboule?"

"Yes, little baron, a wonder," she repeated: "the Little Man with the Frozen Smile."

"Little Man with the Frozen Smile?" I echoed.

"Come and see, come and see, little baron!" cried Schneeboule, hurrying on ahead.

In a few moments we had reached the grotto and bounded into it with the Princess leading the way.

Suddenly she halted in front of a magnificent block of crystal ice, clear as polished glass, and cried out,—

"There, look! There is the Little Man with the Frozen Smile!"

Even now, as the thought of that moment comes over me, I feel something of the thrill of half fear, half joy, as my eyes fell upon the little creature shut in that superb block of ice, himself a part of it, himself its heart, its contents, its mystery. There, in its centre, in easy posture, with wide opened eyes, and with what might be called a smile upon its face—that is a glint of kindliness and affection in its strange eyes with their overhanging brows, sat a small animal of the chimpanzee race. He had possibly been asleep when the icy flood struck him, dreaming of beautiful trees bending beneath purple fruit, of cloudless skies above and a coral beach below, and death had come to him so quickly that he had become a brother to this block of ice while the happy dream was still in his thoughts.

THE LITTLE MAN WITH THE FROZEN SMILE.

It was wonderful, it was more than wonderful! Spellbound by the strange spectacle, I stood there, I know not how long, with my eyes looking into his. At last Schneeboule's voice aroused me:

"Ha! ha!" she laughed; "look, little baron, Bulger is trying to kiss his poor dead brother."

In truth, Bulger did have his nose pressed firmly against the block of ice in his effort to scent the strange animal imprisoned in that crystal cell—so near, and yet so far beyond the reach of his keen scent.

"Well, little baron," cried Schneeboule, "did I not speak truly? Have I not shown thee the Little Man with the Frozen Smile?"

"Indeed thou hast, fair princess," was my reply; "and I cannot tell thee how grateful I am to thee for having done so."

Then, as she plucked me by the sleeve, I pleaded, "Nay, gentle Schneeboule, not yet, not yet, let me bide a bit longer. The Little Man with the Frozen Smile seems to beg me not to go. I can almost imagine that I hear him whisper: 'O little baron, break open the crystal cell of my prison and take me with thee back to the world of sunshine, back to the land of the orange-tree, where the soft warm winds used to rock me to sleep in the cradle of the swaying boughs, while the wise and watchful patriarch of our flock stood guard over us all.'"

Schneeboule's big, round, gray eyes filled with tears at these words.

"Would that he were alive, little baron," she murmured, "and that I could give him some of my happiness to pay him back for all the long years he has been spending in his icy prison."

In a few moments Schneeboule took me by the hand and led me away from the great block of ice with its silent prisoner. My heart was very heavy, and both Schneeboule and Bulger did their utmost to divert me, but all to no purpose.

Leaving the princess at the portal of the palace, I went to my dwelling which was ablaze with the soft glow of its alabaster lamps, and there I found a beautiful new pelt spread over my divan, a new gift from King Gelidus. But I could take no pleasure in it. My thoughts were all with the Little Man with the Frozen Smile locked in the icy embrace of that crystal mould, which, in its cold irony, let him seem to be so free and unfettered and yet held him in such vise-like grip. After a while I dismissed my serving people and laid me down for the night with my dear Bulger nestled against my breast. But I could not sleep. All night long those strange eyes with their uncanny glint followed me about, pleading strong but silent for me to come again, for me to soften my heart like a child of the sunshine that I was, to shatter his crystal dungeon, and set him loose, to bear him away from the icy domain of the Koltykwerps out into the warm air of the upper world. What was I dreaming about? Was he not dead? Had not his spirit left his body thousands and thousands of years ago? Why should I let such wild thoughts vex my mind? What good would come of it? None, none whatever. I was a reasonable creature, I must not give lodgment within my brain to such silly ideas.

The Little Man with the Frozen Smile had been, through almost playful fate, laid away in a beautiful tomb. I must not disturb it. No doubt in his lifetime he had been the pet of a noble manor, brought to the Northland from some sunny clime by master of powerful argosy. Let him rest in peace. I must not dare to mar the beauty of his crystal tomb, so gloriously transparent!

I was even sorry that Schneeboule had led me into her beautiful grotto, and resolved to go thither no more.

What poor weak creatures are we, so fertile in good resolutions and yet so unfruitful of results, planting whole acres with fair promises, but when the tender shoots pierce the ground turning our back upon the crop as if it didn't belong to us!

CHAPTER XXV

A SLEEPLESS NIGHT FOR BULGER AND ME AND WHAT FOLLOWED IT.—INTERVIEW WITH KING GELIDUS.—MY REQUEST AND HIS REPLY.—WHAT ALL TOOK PLACE WHEN I LEARNED THAT THE KING AND HIS COUNCILLORS HAD DECIDED NOT TO GRANT MY REQUEST.—STRANGE TUMULT AMONG THE KOLTYKWERPS, AND HOW HIS FRIGID MAJESTY STILLED IT, AND SOME OTHER THINGS.

Not only had I been unable to sleep, but by my tossing about I had kept poor dear Bulger awake so that when morning came we both looked haggard enough. I felt as if I had been through a fit of sickness, and no doubt he did too. At any rate I had no appetite for the heavy meat diet of the Koltykwerps, and seeing me refuse my breakfast, Bulger did likewise.

I had promised Schneeboule to come early to the palace, for she had a number of questions which she wished to ask me concerning the upper world.

"Good-morning, little baron," she cried in her sweetest tones as I entered the throne-room. "Didst sleep well last night on the new pelt which papa sent thee?" I was about to make a reply when Schneeboule's hand coming in contact with mine,—for we had both removed our gloves in order to shake hands,—she uttered a piercing scream, and drawing back stood there blowing her breath on her right palm as she exclaimed, again and again,—

"Firebrand! Firebrand!"

In an instant King Gelidus and a group of his councillors drew near, and, pulling over their gloves, one after the other laid his hand in mine.

"Glowing coals!" cried his frigid Majesty.

"Tongue of flame!" roared Phrostyphiz.

"Boiling water!" groaned Glacierbhoy.

"Red hot!" hissed Icikul.

"Thou must leave the palace at once," half pleaded King Gelidus. "It would simply he madness for me to permit such a firebrand to remain within the walls of the royal residence. The intense heat of thy body would be sure to melt a hole in its walls ere the sun goes down."

The royal councillors again drew off their gloves and laid hands upon poor Bulger, when a second alarm, even wilder than the first, was sent up and we were hastily escorted back to our lodging-house.

No doubt, dear friends, you will be somewhat mystified upon reading these words, but the explanation is easy: Owing to worriment and lack of sleep, Bulger and I had awaked in a highly feverish condition, and to the Koltykwerps we had really seemed to be almost on fire, but our fever left us toward night; hearing which, King Gelidus sent for us and did all in his power to entertain us with song and dance, in both of which, Schneeboule was very skilled. Finding that his frigid Majesty was in such a rosy humor, if I may be allowed to speak that way of a person whose face was almost as white as the alabaster lamps over his head, I determined to ask him for permission to cleave asunder the icy cell of the Little Man with the Frozen Smile, and ascertain if possible from the collar, which, made up apparently of gold and silver coin was clasped around his neck, to whom he had belonged and where his home had been.

No sooner had I proferred my request, than I noticed that the white face of the royal Gelidus parted with its smile and took on a terribly icy look.

Methought I could look through the tip of his nose as though an icicle, and methought, too, that his ears shone in the light of the alabaster lamps like sheets of crystal ice, and that his voice as he spoke puffed into my face like the first flakes of a coming snowstorm.

I quickly repented me of my rash action. But it was too late and I determined to stand by it.

"Little baron," spoke royal Gelidus in icy tones, "never a heart beat in a kingly breast that was purer and colder than mine, freer from the warmth of selfishness, with not a single hot corner for ire or anger to nestle in, or for weakness or folly to make their hiding-places. For thousands of years my people have inhabited this icy domain and breathed this pure cold air, and never yet hath one desired to strike an axe of flint into the walls of that crystal prison. However, little baron, there may be some warm corner in my heart wherein cold and limpid wisdom may not be at home. Therefore, come to me to-morrow for my answer, meanwhile I'll take council with the coolest brains and coldest hearts about me. If they see no harm in thy request, thou mayst crack open the crystal gates that have for so many centuries shut the manlike creature in his silent cell, and take him forth in order to study the mystic words graven on his collar; but upon the strict condition that in cleaving open his house of crystal my quarry men so apply their wedges of flint as to break the block into two equal pieces, that when thou hast read what may be there, the two parts be closed upon the little man again, edge fitting edge, like a perfect mould, so exactly that to the eye no sign of line or joint be visible. Dost promise, little baron, that this shall be as to our royal will, it seems meet that it should be?"

I promised most solemnly that the crystal cell of the Little Man with the Frozen Smile should be opened and closed exactly as his frigid Majesty had directed.

It would be hard for me to tell you, dear friends, how happy I went to rest that night upon my icy divan, and how as the tiny flame of my alabaster lamp shed its soft glow upon the walls of ice, I lay there turning over in my mind the strange and mysterious pleasure which was soon to fall to my lot when the quarry men of King Gelidus should set their wedges of flint in this glorious block of ice and cleave it asunder.

Even Don Fum, Master of Masters, had never dreamed of receiving a message from the people who lived in the very childhood of the world, and in anticipation already I enjoyed the splendid triumph which would be mine when I came to lecture before learned societies upon the mysterious lettering on the curious collar clasping the neck of the Little Man with the Frozen Smile.

Imagine my anguish then, dear friends, upon receiving a message from King Gelidus the next day that his councillors had with one voice decreed against the opening of the crystal prison which stood in Schneeboule's grotto!

I was as if smitten with some sudden and awful ailment. I had never felt until that moment how keen the tooth of disappointment could be. I shivered first with a chill that made me brother to the Koltykwerps, and then I burned with a fever so raging that a wild rumor spread through Gelidus' icy domain that I was setting fire to the very walls and roof. With wild outcries, and faces drawn with nameless dread, the subjects of his frigid Majesty rushed pell mell up the wide flights of stairs leading to the palace of ice, and pleaded for the king to show himself.

In cold and frigid majesty, Gelidus walked out upon the platform and listened to the prayers of his people.

"We shall burn," they cried; "our beautiful homes will fall about our ears. These crystal steps will melt away, and all these fair columns and arches and statues and pedestals will turn to water and empty themselves into the lower caverns of the earth. The great window of our sky will fall with awful crash upon our heads, putting an end forever to this fair domain of crystal splendor. O Gelidus, haste thee, haste thee, ere it be too late, let the little baron have his way before bitter disappointment transforms his body and limbs into tongues of flame to lick up this magnificent palace in a single night, and dash its thousand alabaster lamps to the ground, a heap of sheards, no fragment matching its brother fragment, but all a wretched mass of worthless matter!"

King Gelidus and his frosty councillors saw that it would be useless to attempt to reason with the people, and therefore turning toward them, he coldly waved his chilly right hand, and with an icy smile spoke frostily as follows,—

"Go, Koltykwerps to your homes, and be happy. What think you, have I a heated brain, doth my heart steam with foolishness, that you should think me capable of wishing harm to the tiniest Koltykwerp that spins his top of ice in my fair kingdom? Go to your homes, I say; the little baron is already cooling off, for he hath my full consent to cleave asunder the crystal prison of the Little Man with the Frozen Smile. There is nothing be frightened about, my children. So eat hearty suppers and sleep soundly to-night, for my royal word for it, by to-morrow morning the little baron will cease to be the least bit dangerous to the peace and welfare of our icy kingdom. A cold good-night to you all."

In a short half hour the panic-stricken Koltykwerps were all back in their homes again, and when a messenger came from King Gelidus to measure my temperature he found such a great improvement that he opened his chilly heart and sent me a beautiful present from his treasure house, to wit: A small block of ice, clearer than any gem I had ever seen, in the heart of which lay a glorious red rose in fullest bloom, each velvet petal opened out eagerly. Upon consulting my diary I found that it was just six months to a day since I had left Castle Trump and the loved ones sheltered by its time-worn tiles, and cold as was the covering of this thrice beautiful child of the upper world I clasped it to my breast and shed tears.

And this was the way it came about, dear friends, that King Gelidus and his frosty councillors were brought to give their consent to my cleaving asunder the icy prison wherein lay the Little Man with the Frozen Smile.

CHAPTER XXVI

HOW THE QUARRY MEN OF KING GELIDUS CLEFT ASUNDER THE CRYSTAL PRISON OF THE LITTLE MAN WITH THE FROZEN SMILE.—MY BITTER DISAPPOINTMENT, AND HOW I BORE IT.—WONDERFUL HAPPENINGS OF THE NIGHT THAT FOLLOWED.—BULGER AGAIN PROVES HIMSELF TO BE AN ANIMAL OF EXTRAORDINARY SAGACITY.

Bulger and I had little appetite for the dainty breakfast of stewed sweetbreads which the Koltykwerps set before us the next morning, for I knew, and he half suspected, that something important was going to happen, being nothing less than the cleaving asunder of the crystal cell which had held the little chimpanzee a prisoner for so many centuries.

Walking beside the merry Princess Schneeboule, who was delighted to know that his frigid Majesty, her father, had at last yielded to my wishes, Bulger and I set out for the beautiful ice grotto; behind us walked Phrostyphiz and Glacierbhoy with instructions from the king to supervise the cleaving asunder of the block of ice; and after them came four of King Gelidus' quarry men, two bearing flint axes with helves of polished bone, and two carrying the flint wedges to be used in the work.

We soon entered Schneeboule's grotto, and the task was at once entered upon.

It seemed to me I could almost see the Little Man with the Frozen Smile wink his eyelids as the quarry men set their wedges in place and began to mark the line of fracture; but, of course, dear friends, you know what an imagination I have, especially when I get worked up over anything. So you must take what I say sometimes with a grain of salt, although as a rule, you may accept my statements with child-like confidence.

With such wonderful skill did the Koltykwerpian quarry men use their axes and wedges that in a few moments, to my great delight, the huge block of ice fell asunder in perfect halves, in one of which the little manlike creature lay on his side like a casting in a mould.

I made haste to lift him out and wrap him a soft pelt, which I had brought along for that purpose, and then I turned to retrace my steps to my chamber, where I intended to begin at once my study of whatever inscriptions should be found upon his curious collar.

"Remember little baron," said Glacierbhoy, "by express command of his frigid Majesty, the Little Man with the Frozen Smile must be returned to his crystal cell to-morrow morning at this very hour."

I bowed assent, and then, having accompanied Princess Schneeboule as far as the bottom of the grand staircase leading to the ice palace, I turned away and was soon in the privacy of my own apartment.

Now came for me one of the bitterest disappointments of my life; but I submitted with a good grace, for it was fit punishment visited upon me for my foolish vanity in striving to unearth some older record of the human race than had yet been done by any of the great searchers and philosophers, not even excepting that Master of Masters, Don Strephalofidgeguaneriusfum!

Know then, dear friends, that the quaint collar, made up of gold and silver coins, or disks, cunningly linked together, which encircled the animal's neck, contained not a single word or letter of any language, the undersides being quite blank, and the upper merely having roughly carved outlines of an object which might possibly have been intended for the sun.

Wrapping the animal up in the soft pelt, I laid him away in a corner of my divan and betook myself to the palace of his frigid Majesty, where I frankly informed King Gelidus of my great disappointment in not finding some few words or even a single word of a language unknown to the wisest heads of the upper world.

Schneeboule was so touched by my sadness that, had I not skilfully kept out of her way, I verily believe she would have thrown her arms around my neck and imprinted upon my cheek the kiss which would have made me the king of the Koltykwerps; but I had no longing to spend the rest of my life in the icy domains of his frigid Majesty, even though my brow would be crowned with the cold crown of the Koltykwerps. If I had been an old man, with slow and feeble pulse, it would have been very different; but my heart was too warm and my blood too hot to fill such a position with agreeableness to myself or satisfaction to the people of this icy under world. So I kept the little princess busy enough, I can assure you, first with songs, then with dance, and then with story-telling.

That night King Gelidus ordered a magnificent fête to be held in my honor. Five hundred more alabaster lamps were lighted, and the royal divans were laid with the richest pelts in the palace, and after the dancing and singing had ended, frozen tidbits from the royal kitchen were passed around on alabaster salvers, and Bulger and I ate until our teeth ached.

It was late when we reached our own apartment, and so full were my thoughts of the beautiful sights which we had gazed upon in the throne-room, that I had quite forgotten about the poor Little Man with the Frozen Smile whom I had covered up and tucked away on my divan; but Bulger had not been so hard-hearted.

Twenty times during the evening he had given me a sly tug at my sleeve as much as to say,—

BULGER SHOWS THE BARON SOMETHING WONDERFUL.

"Come, little master, let's hurry back; dost not remember that we left my poor little frozen brother tucked away in that icy chamber all alone by himself?" I was very weary and I fell off to sleep almost immediately, and yet I had an indistinct recollection that Bulger was not in his place against my breast. I remembered feeling for him, but that's all. It never flashed upon me that he had gone and lain down beside the poor little stranger, whom I had so unfeelingly lifted from his last resting-place, and yet such must have been the case, for about midnight, it seemed to me, I was awakened by a gentle tugging at my sleeve.

It was my faithful Bulger, but, half awake and half asleep as I was, I merely thought that he was only asking for a caress, as was often his wont when he fell a-thinking about home, so I reached out and stroked his head several times and dropped off again.

But the tugging began anew, and this time 'twas more vigorous and with it came an impatient whine which meant,—

"Come, come, little master, rouse thee; dost suppose I would break thy rest unless there were good reasons for it?" I didn't need a third reminder, but with a single bound landed on my feet, and reaching out for one of the tiny tapers which the Koltykwerps make use of as lighters, I carried the flames from the single lamp burning on the wall to the three others hanging here and there.

The icy walls of my chamber were now ablaze with light. There sat Bulger on the fur-covered divan, beside the place where the Little Man with the Frozen Smile lay hidden under the pelt. His tail was wagging nervously, and his large, lustrous eyes were fixed first upon me and then upon the covering of his dead brother with an expression I never remembered having seen in them before, and then with a sudden movement he laid hold of the pelt and, drawing it aside, showed me, what think you, dear friends, what, I ask in a tone half whisper, half gasp, for now years after I still can feel that wonderful thrill which I felt then? Why, it was alive! That ape-like creature had come to life after his sleep of thousands of years in that narrow, crystal cell! Bulger had lain down beside his frozen brother and warmed him back to life again!

Oh, it was wondrously wonderful to see that pair of little eyes, beadlike in brightness, look up and blink at me; and then to hear that low, moaning voice, so human-like, as if it whimpered, with a shake and a shiver,—

"Oh, how cold it is! how very cold it is! Where's the sun? Where's the soft warm wind, and where are the cloudless skies so blue, oh so beautifully blue, that used to hang over my head?"

Bidding Bulger lie down again beside him and snuggle up as close as possible, I made haste to cover them both with the softest skins I could find.

In a few moments there came from underneath the pile a low, contented cry of "Coojah! Coojah! Coojah!" followed by a curious addition sounding like "Fuff! Fuff! Fuff!" so I put them all together and named the strange new comer to the icy domain of King Gelidus—Fuffcoojah!

Sleep any more that night? Not a wink. The same joy came over me that I used to feel on Christmas morning long ago when Kris Kringle brought me some wonderful bit of mechanism moved by a secret spring—for I always scorned to accept ordinary toys like ordinary children; and oh, how I longed for the morning, when it would be time for me to bundle up the Little Man—no longer him with the Frozen Smile, but Fuffcoojah, the Live Boy from

Faraway, with his curious little face screwed up into such a funny look—and carry him to the palace.

How delighted Schneeboule will be! thought I, and King Gelidus too, how he will unbend from his frigid majesty as he watches the antics of Fuffcoojah, and how pleased all the dignified Koltykwerpians, including even Phrostyphiz and Glacierbhoy, will be when I tell them that the Little Man with the Frozen Smile has come to life again!

What crowds of Koltykwerps, men, women and children, will rush up the long flights of steps leading to the Ice Palace, begging and entreating King Gelidus to let them have just a little look at Fuffcoojah, the little man set free from his icy cell by the famous traveller, Baron Sebastian von Troomp!

CHAPTER XXVII

EXCITEMENT OVER FUFFCOOJAH.—I CARRY HIM TO THE COURT OF KING GELIDUS.—HIS INSTANT AFFECTION FOR PRINCESS SCHNEEBOULE.—I AM ACCUSED OF EXERCISING THE BLACK ART.—MY DEFENCE AND MY REWARD.—ANXIETY OF THE KOLTYKWERPS LEST FUFFCOOJAH PERISH OF HUNGER.—THIS CALAMITY AVERTED, ANOTHER STARES US IN THE FACE: HOW TO KEEP HIM FROM FREEZING TO DEATH.—I SOLVE THE PROBLEM, BUT DRAW UPON ME A STRANGE MISFORTUNE.

It all turned out just as I had thought it would! The moment it became known that the Little Man with the Frozen Smile had actually come to life, the wildest excitement prevailed in every part of the icy domain of his frigid Majesty. I was astounded at the change in the actions of the Koltykwerps. They moved more quickly, they talked faster, they made more gestures than I had ever seen them do before. In some cases, you will hardly believe it, dear friends, I actually noticed a faint glow in the cold cheeks of a few of them.

I had hoped to be able to bundle Fuffcoojah up warmly and make my escape to the ice palace before the people learned of his coming to life, but in vain. When I made my appearance at the door, there was a large crowd of Koltykwerps pushing and pulling in front of my quarters.

Most of them were good-natured, and cried out,—

"Show him to us, little baron, show us the Little Man with the Frozen Smile whom thou hast brought to life. Let us look upon his face!"

"Nay, nay, Koltykwerps!" I exclaimed, "it must not be! His frigid Majesty must be the first to look upon Fuffcoojah's face. Room, room for the noble guest of royal Gelidus! In the name of his frigid Majesty give way and let me pass!"

The Koltykwerps showed no inclination to obey. To such a pitch of excitement had they worked themselves up that only upon seeing Bulger advance upon them with flashing eye and teeth laid bare, did they reach the conclusion that my brave companion was in no mood to be trifled with.

Thwarted in their wild desire to get a peep at Fuffcoojah, the Koltykwerps now began to rail at me as I passed them by on my way to the ice palace.

"Oho, Master magician! Ha, ha, Prince of the Black Art! Boo, boo, little wizard! Have a care, wily necromancer, see to it that thou dost not practise any of thy tricks of enchantment upon us!" I was glad when the axe-bearer saw my plight and hurried forward to extricate me from the crowd of angry people.

King Gelidus met me at the portal of his ice palace, and at his heels came Princess Schneeboule, who could hardly wait for her turn to take a look at the curious living creature which I unwrapped just enough to let her see its nose.

The instant Fuffcoojah set eyes upon the sweet face of the Koltykwerpian princess, he stretched out his little arm as a child might to its mother. This sudden show of affection caused Schneeboule the liveliest pleasure, and quickly drawing off one of her gloves she reached out and stroked the animal's head, but at the touch of those, to him, icy little fingers he uttered a low wail and drew back underneath the warm pelt in which he was snugly wrapped.

Poor Schneeboule! she gave a sigh as she saw him do this, but it didn't prevent her from coming every minute or so and lifting one end of the pelt just enough to take another look at Fuffcoojah, who, while he never failed to cuddle up closer to me at sight of the princess, yet invariably thrust out one of his black paws from under the pelt for Schneeboule to shake. While seated on the divan nearest the throne, I observed that Phrostyphiz and Glacierbhoy were holding a whispered conference with his frigid Majesty. At once I guessed the subject of their conversation.

Rising to my feet, I made a sign that I wished to address the king, and when he had nodded his head with stern and icy dignity, I began to speak. You know, dear friends, how eloquent I can be when the mood is upon me. Well, standing there almost upon the steps of King Gelidus' throne of ice, I proceeded to defend myself against the charge of being a master of the black art. I will not tell you all I said, but this was my ending:

"May it please your frigid Majesty!

"Here beside me stands the only magician in the case, and the only art, the only trick or charm which was exercised by him was that sweet power we call love. When first he set eyes upon his four-footed brother locked in the crystal cell of Schneeboule's Grotto, he pressed his nose again and again against its icy wall in vain attempt to know his kinsman, and turned away with a cry of sorrow to find that his keen scent could not penetrate to him. I cannot tell you how great was his joy when I laid Fuffcoojah stiff and stark upon my divan, for I knew not then the scheme ripening in Bulger's mind. But later, all was plain enough. The loving dog leaves his master's breast and carries his true and tender heart over to where Fuffcoojah lies, raises the pelt, crawls in beside him, and presses his warm breast firm and hard against his brother's ice-locked heart, and warms him into life again, then wakes me and tells me what he hath done.

"This, Royal Gelidus and most noble Koltykwerps, is the only art that hath been used to bring Fuffcoojah back to life again, and to call it black is to slander the sunshine, rail at the lily, and call the sweet breath of heaven a vile and detestable thing!"

When I had ended my speech I saw that Schneeboule had been weeping, and that several of her tears stopped in their course down her cheeks hung there sparkling like tiny diamonds in the soft light of the alabaster lamps, where the chill air of Gelidus' palace had turned them into ice.

And therefore when his frigid Majesty said that my words had touched his heart, and bade me ask for a gift from his hand, I said,—

"O cold king of this fair icy domain, let those tears that now hang like tiny jewels on Schneeboule's cheeks be brushed into an alabaster box and given to me. I covet no other guerdon!"

"Even if I did not love thee, little baron," cried King Gelidus with an icy smile, "I would be persuaded; but loving makes easy believing. Go, Phrostyphiz, and bid one of the princess's women brush those tiny jewels that hang on Schneeboule's cheek into an alabaster cup and bestow them upon the little baron."

Scarcely had this been done when Fuffcoojah thrust his head out from under the pelt and, fixing his eyes pleadingly upon me, thrust out his tongue and opened and shut his mouth with a faint, smacking noise. Quick as a flash it dawned upon me that these signs meant that Fuffcoojah was hungry!

And then, as I suddenly remembered that the Koltykwerps were strictly a meat-eating people, that only meat was to be had in their chill domain, quarried almost like marble itself from nature's great refrigerators, a gasp escaped my lips, and I whispered,—

"Oh, he must die! He must die!" My words had not missed the keen ears of Princess Schneeboule.

"Speak, little baron," she cried, "why, why, must little Fuffcoojah die? What dost mean by such a saying?" And when King Gelidus and Schneeboule had heard me voice my fear that he would die rather than feed on meat, they both became very heavy-hearted.

"Poor little Fuffcoojah!" moaned the princess, "can it be possible that he must be carried back so soon to his crystal cell in my grotto?"

"Bid the master of my meat quarries approach the throne," cried King Gelidus suddenly, in a voice of icy dignity.

This important functionary soon made his appearance.

Turning to me, the king bade me explain the case to him. This I did in a few words, when, to the great joy of all present the master of the meat quarries spoke as follows:—

"Little baron, if that's the only trouble, give thyself no further uneasiness, for I shall at once send one of my men to thee with a supply of most delicious nuts."

"Delicious nuts?" I repeated in a tone of amazement.

"Why, yes, little baron, I have a goodly supply on hand. Know, then, that hardly a day goes by that my men don't come upon some fine specimen of the family of gnawers, most generally squirrels, in whose cheek-pouches we invariably find from one to half a dozen dainty nuts stowed away. It has always been my custom to lay these aside, and so I have to inform thee that if Fuffcoojah should live to be a hundred years old I or my successor could guarantee to keep him supplied with food."

These words lifted a terrible load off my heart, for now, at least, Fuffcoojah would not die of starvation.

For a few days everything went well. The Koltykwerps became quite satisfied in their own minds that I had not been practising the black art in the chilly kingdom of his frigid Majesty, and each and every one of them became greatly attached to the curious little creature with the droll little face and droller manner.

But it seemed as if we were no sooner out of one trouble than we were plumped into another, for now Fuffcoojah began to object to the attendant selected to look after him by King Gelidus.

The man was about ten degrees too cold-blooded for him, and ere long it was only necessary for the Koltykwerp to approach Fuff,—as we called him for short,—in order to throw him into convulsions of shivering and to cause him to utter pitiable cries of discontent, which only ceased upon my appearing and comforting him by my caresses.

I now set to work to devise some way to make Fuff's life more agreeable to him, for everybody seemed to hold me responsible for his well being. Ten times a day came messengers from King Gelidus or from Princess Schneeboule to ask how he was getting on, and whether we were keeping him warm enough, whether he had all he wanted to eat, whether he had pelts enough on his bed. Nor was it an unusual thing to have a score or more Koltykwerpian mothers call at my quarters during a single day with advice enough to last a month, and therefore was it that, with a view to providing him with a warmer room to sleep in, I ordered a divan fitted up for him in a smaller chamber opening into mine, upon the walls of which I directed half a dozen of the largest lamps to be hung.

The consequence was that the walls began to melt, hearing of which, consternation spread throughout the icy domain of his frigid Majesty, for to the mind of a Koltykwerp heat powerful enough to melt ice was something terrible. It was like the dread of earthquake shock to us, or the fear of flood or flame. It was something that filled their hearts with such terror that in their dreams they saw the solid walls of the ice palace melt asunder and fall with a crash. They could not bear it, and so King Gelidus put forth the decree that if there were no other way to keep Fuffcoojah alive, then must he die.

Hearing this, an awful grief came upon poor Schneeboule's heart, for she had learned to love little Fuff very dearly, and it set a knife in her breast to think of losing him.

"Never, never," she cried, "shall I be able to set foot within my grotto if Fuffcoojah is put back into his crystal prison again, with his frozen smile on his face as once used to be." And seeking out her royal father she threw herself at his knees and spoke as follows:—

"O heart of ice! O frigid Majesty, let not thy child die of grief. There is an easy way out of all our trouble with dear little Fuffcoojah."

"Speak, beloved Schneeboule," answered King Gelidus, "let me hear what it is."

"Why, cold heart," said the princess, "the little baron hath plenty of warmth stored away in his body, he hath enough for both himself and Fuffcoojah into the bargain. Therefore, frigid father, command that a deep, warm hood be made to the little baron's coat, and that Fuffcoojah be placed therein and be borne about by the little baron wherever he goeth. He will soon grow accustomed to the slender burden and note it no more."

"It shall be as thou wishest," replied the king of the Koltykwerps; and calling his trusty councillor, Glacierbhoy, he directed him to summon me at once to the throne-room. When I heard this terrible order issue from the icy lips of King Gelidus my heart sank within me, and yet I dared not disobey, I dared not murmur, for I it was who had cleft asunder the crystal prison of the Little Man with the Frozen Smile; I who had made it possible for Bulger to warm him back to life again. Oh, poor, vain, weak, foolish boy that I had been, what was to become of me now?

CHAPTER XXVIII

HOW A LITTLE BURDEN MAY GROW TO BE A GRIEVOUS ONE.—STORY OF A MAN WITH A MONKEY IN HIS HOOD.—MY TERRIBLE SUFFERING.—CONCERNING THE AWFUL PANIC THAT SEIZED UPON THE KOLTYKWERPS.—MY VISIT TO THE DESERTED ICE-PALACE, AND WHAT HAPPENED TO FUFFCOOJAH.—END OF HIS BRIEF BUT STRANGE CAREER.—A FROZEN KISS ON A BLADE OF HORN, OR HOW SCHNEEBOULE CHOSE A HUSBAND.

Ah, little princess, how easy was it for thee to say that I would soon grow accustomed to the slender burden and note it no more? How prone are we to call light the burdens which we lay upon the shoulders of others for our own benefit? True, Fuffcoojah was not as long as a horse, nor as broad as an ox, and when in accordance with the king's decree the hood had been completed and the little animal was stowed away therein, close against my back so as to get a goodly share of the warmth of my body, it seemed to me that Schneeboule was right, that I would soon become accustomed to the load and note it no more. And so it seemed the second and the third day, but not on the fourth; for on that day the little load appeared to have gained somewhat in weight, and although I was quick to feign that it was not so when Princess Schneeboule quizzed me saying,—

"There, little baron, did I not tell thee that thou wouldst soon forget that Fuffcoojah slept upon thy shoulders?" yet in my heart I felt that he really had grown a mite heavier.

On the fifth day Bulger and I were bidden to a merry-making at the palace of ice, and as I rose from my divan to betake me thither, methought I was strangely heavy-hearted, and so did Bulger, for he made several efforts to draw a smile, or a cheery tone, from me, but in vain.

THE BARON'S FLIGHT TO THE ICE PALACE.

Suddenly I realized that there was a weight pressing against my back, no, not a heavy weight, but a weight all the same, and then I whispered to myself, "Why, if I am going to a merry-making, I'll cast it off!" and then I wakened from my deep abstraction and murmured,—

"How strange that I should have forgotten that Fuffcoojah was in my hood?" And so I went to the merry-making with Fuffcoojah nestled between my shoulders, and the Koltykwerps laughed at the little baron and his child, as they called him, and drew near and raised the flap and peeped in at the curious creature within the hood, and when Fuffcoojah felt their icy breaths, he buried his nose in the fur and sighed and whimpered. Then, for a moment, when the Princess Schneeboule came and sat beside me and praised me for my readiness to carry out her wishes, and thanked me so sweetly for my goodness to her, I forgot all about the little load laid upon me, and I ate the frozen tidbits from the royal kitchen, and laughed and joked with Lords Phrostyphiz and Glacierbhoy, just as had been my wont before Gelidus had decreed that Fuffcoojah should make his bed on my shoulders.

But when the fête was over and I stepped from the broad portal of the ice-palace and looked up at the mighty lens set in the mountain side, through which the moonlight of the outer world was streaming in subdued but glorious splendor, I suddenly felt my legs bend under me, I staggered from right to left, I clutched at shadows, I was, it seemed to me, about to be crushed beneath a terrible burden. I quickened my pace, I broke into a run, I threw my arms into the air as if I would cast off the weight that was smothering me. And so I came to my lodging puffing, panting, gasping.

"Why, what a fool am I!" was my first word when I had got my breath; "it's only little Fuffcoojah on my back, stowed away in my fur hood. I must be beside myself to have thought that a great monster was seated there and that he was gradually pressing me down, crushing the life out of me by degrees, flattening me to the very ground, and I not able to escape from his terrible embrace or to squirm out from under his awful limbs wrapt around my neck and body!"

All night long this monster was clinging to me, and urging me to a faster pace, up and down, across and around, I knew not where, on bootless errands, ending only to begin again, on searches after nothing hidden nowhere, trying a thousand lids and finding every one locked, returning home only to go forth again, up and away and out on interminable highways vanishing in a point far on ahead, with that grievous burden forever on my shoulders growing heavier and heavier, till it seemed that I must go down with it into the dust. But no, it knew full well that it must not ride me to the death, so when I was ready to drop, it threw off part of its weight to give me courage to begin again. When the morning came my pulse was galloping and my cheeks were on fire. I could feel the blood pounding against my temples, and it was natural that my face should be crimsoned over with the flush of fever. Half in a daze I walked forth toward the grand staircase leading up to the ice palace, when suddenly I was startled by a fearful scream. I halted and looked up, when another and another burst upon my ears.

The terrified Koltykwerps were fleeing before me in every direction, shrieking as they fled,—

"Fly, fly, brothers, the little baron is burning, the little baron is burning, fly, brothers, fly!"

In a few moments terror had seized upon every living creature in the icy domain of King Gelidus. They fled from me in mad haste, taking refuge in the distant caverns and corridors, filling the air with their wild outcries, no one being brave enough to halt and take a second look. My inflamed countenance filled them with such awful terror that they could only tear along and cry,—

"Fly, brothers, fly; the little baron is burning, the little baron is burning!"

With Bulger at my heels, I turned and sprang up the staircase with the intention of seeking out King Gelidus, and explaining the matter to him.

But he, too, had fled, and with him every sentinel and serving man, every courtier and councillor. The palace was as still as death. I hastened through its silent corridors calling out,—

"Schneeboule! Princess Schneeboule! Surely thou art not afraid of me? Turn back, I will not harm thee, I'm not burning! Turn back, oh, turn back!"

With this, I reached the throne-room; not a living creature was to be seen; the vast chamber was as still as death. I staggered to a divan, and pillowing my poor aching head on a cushion, I fell into a sound and refreshing sleep.

When I awoke, I rubbed my eyes and looked about me, and at first I thought that I was still alone in the great round chamber with its walls of ice; but no, there on the divan sat Schneeboule, and she smiled and said in mock displeasure,—

"Thou art not a very watchful nurse, little baron, for in thy sleep thou didst squeeze Fuffcoojah so tightly against a cushion, that he crawled out from thy hood and nestled in my arms."

"In thy arms, Schneeboule?" I exclaimed breathlessly, for I feared for the worst, and springing up I drew aside the soft pelt which she had wrapped around Fuffcoojah, and there he lay, dead! Poor little beast, he had been so happy to crawl into the arms of one he loved so dearly, and had cuddled up closer and closer to her in search of greater warmth; but only to come nearer and nearer to a heart that could not warm him; and so the insidious chill of death, which bringeth sweet and pleasant drowsiness with it, had stole over him and he had died.

And Schneeboule's tears, freezing as they fell, now showered like a gentle hail of tiny gems upon the little dead beast, no longer Fuffcoojah, but once again the Little Man with the Frozen Smile. Presently the Koltykwerps recovered from their senseless fear, and first one by one, and then group-wise, they returned to their homes, King Gelidus and his court coming back too, to the fair palace which they had abandoned in their wild fright when the cry had gone up that the little baron was burning.

Everybody was sorry to hear that Fuffcoojah had died the second time, and many were the frozen tears that dropped from the chilly cheeks of the Koltykwerps as they looked upon the Little Man with the Frozen Smile as he lay on the white pelt beside the Princess Schneeboule.

That day we bore him back to the ice grotto, and having laid him in the hollow moulded by his body in the crystal block, it was closed again so skilfully by the king's quarrymen that no eye was keen enough to note where the cleavage had been. And the same uncanny glint was in his eyes, and when the Koltykwerps saw this their icy hearts felt a cold shiver of satisfaction, for not only was the Little Man with the Frozen Smile back in his crystal cell again, but all the fears and dreadful fancies which his coming to life again had given rise to were past and gone forever, and peace and quiet and sweet contentment reigned throughout the icy realm of his frigid Majesty Gelidus, King of the Koltykwerps!

Now nothing remained to make his cold heart crack with joy but to see his beloved child Schneeboule make choice of a husband. And he had not long to wait, for one day upon entering the palace she saw a youth lying at the foot of the stairway overcome with sleep. In one hand he held an alabaster lamp, and in the other a new wick which he was about to fit into it, for the youth was a lamp-trimmer in the ice palace of King Gelidus; and when the Princess Schneeboule saw him lying there overcome with sleep, she stooped and kissed him on the cheek, and passed on without another thought about the matter, one way or the other.

And the kiss froze on the cheek of the lamp-trimmer, where Schneeboule had pressed it.

DEATH OF FUFFCOOJAH.

Presently King Gelidus came tramping into the hallway with his breath white upon his beard, and he saw the youth lying there, and the frozen kiss on his cheek, and he bade Glacierbhoy scrape the delicate frost crystals from the youth's face with a blade of polished horn.

"What hast there, father of mine?" asked the princess, when she saw him bearing the blade of horn along so carefully.

"A kiss which someone pressed upon the cheek of one of my lamp-trimmers, now lying on the staircase overcome with sleep," replied King Gelidus, in ringing, icy tones.

"Why, father of mine," exclaimed Princess Schneeboule, "now that thou speakest of it, I really believe the kiss is mine, for I recollect kissing someone as I entered the palace, I was deep in thought, but no doubt the youth pleased me as he lay there, asleep with lamp in one hand and wick in the other."

And that lamp-trimmer trimmed no more lamps in the ice palace of his frigid Majesty Gelidus, King of the Koltykwerps.

No doubt he made Schneeboule a very good husband, and I'm quite sure that she made him a good wife. I would have been glad to tarry for the nuptial feast, but that was out of the question. I had stayed too long already.

CHAPTER XXIX

SOMETHING CONCERNING THE MANY PORTALS TO THE ICY DOMAIN OF KING GELIDUS AND THE DIFFICULT TASK OF CHOOSING THE RIGHT ONE.—HOW BULGER SOLVED IT.—OUR FAREWELL TO THE COLD-BLOODED KOLTYKWERPS.—SCHNEEBOULE'S SORROW AT LOSING US.

As Bullibrain had once remarked, when there are many doors it's a wise man who knows which is the right one to open; and this I found to be the case when I attempted to take my departure from the icy domain of his frigid Majesty, Gelidus, King of the Koltykwerps, for there was a baker's dozen of galleries, in each of which, upon exploring it, I came, after a tramp of half a mile or so, up against a lofty gate of solid ice, curiously carved and fitting the end of the gallery as a cork does a bottle.

No doubt you are wondering why I didn't make my way out of the Koltykwerpian kingdom by following the river: for the very good reason that it went no farther than King Gelidus's domain, emptying into a vast reservoir which apparently had a subterranean outlet, for its thick covering of ice always remained at the same height.

The king's quarrymen were ordered to hew an opening through whichever door I should point out as the one that I wished to pass through, but I was informed by Phrostyphiz that according to the law of the land but one door could be opened during any one year, so that if I found my way blocked and turned back again it would mean a delay of twelve months. Bullibrain, with all his wisdom, was powerless to assist me, although I was half inclined to think that he might have done so had he been permitted to investigate the secret records of the kingdom, carved upon huge tablets of ice, and stored away in the vaults of the palace.

The fact of the matter is King Gelidus was so desirous of having me assist at the marriage feast of Princess Schneeboule, that he threw every obstacle in my way that he could, without openly showing his hand. And Schneeboule herself by the dancing of her clear gray eyes gave me to understand that she, too, was hoping that I would make a mistake when I came to point out the door which I wanted opened.

Bulger saw that I was in trouble, but couldn't comprehend clearly what that trouble was. He kept his eyes fastened upon me, however, watching my every movement, hoping, no doubt, to solve the mystery.

While sitting one day lost in thought over the very serious problem which I found myself called upon to solve, an idea struck me: I had noticed that in the meat-quarries, the workmen often made use of sounding-rods, which were long pieces of polished bone, ending in flint tips. A Koltykwerpian quarryman by dexterously twisting this rod, was able to bore a hole six feet deep or more into the solid bed of ice when desirous of ascertaining the position of a carcass in the meat quarry, and it occurred to me that by piercing the portals of ice which closed their various corridors I have spoken of, possibly Bulger's keen scent might recognize that current of air which would have in it the odor of earth and rock; in other words, make choice for me of the portal which opened on that corridor leading away from the icy domain of King Gelidus and not merely into some outlying chamber of his kingdom.

His frigid Majesty could not object to such experiments, for the law only forbade the hewing of openings large enough for the hewer to pass through.

King Gelidus and half a dozen of his courtiers, looking stern and frigid and conversing in freezing tones, were present to see the experiment tried. Methought their icy lips clacked together with satisfaction when, at my request, one portal after another was pierced, but Bulger, after sniffing at the hole, turned away with a bewildered look in his eyes as if he didn't half understand why I was ordering him to thrust his warm nose into such cold places.

And so we tramped from corridor to corridor, until the quarrymen began to show signs of fatigue, and the sounding-rod turned slower and slower in their hands.

Phrostyphiz blinked his cold gray eyes as much as to say, "Little baron, thou must bide with us for another year!" But I merely turned to the quarrymen, and ordered them to pierce one more portal of ice ere we abandoned the task for the day. They went at the work of piercing the eleventh door with the pace of pack-mules up a mountain-side. But at last the sounding-rod bored a way through, and at a wave of my hand the quarrymen fell back. In an instant Bulger had his nose at the hole, and took three or four quick, nervous sniffs, ending with a long, deep-drawn one, and then breaking out into a string of sharp, jerky, joyful barks, he began scratching furiously at the bottom of the portal.

"Your frigid Majesty," said I, with a low and stately bend of my body such as only those born to the manner can make, "by this portal, at the coming of to-morrow's sun, I shall pass from your Majesty's icy dominion!" And when Phrostyphiz and Glacierbhoy heard these words of mine uttered so loftily, their eyes gleamed cold as steel, and they followed the King in silence back to the palace of ice. Schneeboule met them in the grand hallway; and when she had looked upon their faces she began to weep, for she loved me and she loved Bulger too, and her cold little heart could not bear the thought of our going.

KOLTYKWERPIAN QUARRYMEN HEWING A PASSAGE THROUGH THE WALL OF ICE.

King Gelidus, however, soon recovered his spirits, and ordered a feast with song and dance in honor of Bulger, who during the festivities sat on the highest divan with the softest pelt beneath him; and so many were the frozen tidbits which the Koltykwerps presented to him during the progress of the feast, that I grew alarmed lest he might overload his stomach and not be in a fit condition to make the early start on our journey, of which I had given notice to the Koltykwerpian monarch. But his good sense saved him from doing so foolish a thing; in fact, I was greatly amused to see that, while he accepted every tidbit handed to him, and solemnly went through the motions of chewing it, yet watching his chance, he slyly dropped it out of his mouth and flirted it aside with his paw. Thus was spent our last night at the icy court of his frigid Majesty, and on the morrow the Koltykwerps collected in great crowds on the different terraces to say good-by. I pressed a kiss on the cheek of Princess Schneeboule, and when it had turned to ice crystals, one of her men brushed it into an alabaster box.

Prince Chillychops, the former lamp-trimmer, was on hand with the rest of the Koltykwerpian nobles, but I flattered myself that Schneeboule loved me better than she did him. However, I wished him joy, and gripped his cold palm with such warmth that he stood blowing it for a whole minute. When we reached the lofty portal we found that the quarrymen had already hewn a passage through it, and near by I observed a pile of massive blocks of ice, crystal clear.

These, when Bulger and I should pass through the opening, were to be used in walling it up again; and when I saw this pile of blocks, and remembered the solid workmanship of the Koltykwerpian quarrymen, the thought flitted through my mind: Suppose Bulger hath not chosen wisely, what use would there be in turning back, for my own weak hands would be powerless against a wall built of such blocks, and knock I ever so loud, how could the sound ever traverse this long and winding corridor and reach the ear of a Koltykwerp? "No," said I to myself, "if Bulger hath not chosen wisely, it will be good-by to both upper and under worlds." And then, bearing an alabaster lamp in one hand and in the other holding the cord which I had tied to Bulger's collar, I stepped through the narrow passage hewn by the quarrymen, and turned my back forever on the cold dominion of Gelidus, King of the Koltykwerps. Once I halted and looked back. I could see nothing, but I could hear the sharp click of the flint axes as the quarrymen closed up the door that shut me out from so many cold but loving hearts. And then I drew a long breath and went on my way again.

And that was the last I ever saw of the Koltykwerps save in day dream or night vision.

THE WONDERFUL RIDE ON THE BLOCK OF ICE.

CHAPTER XXX

ALL ABOUT THE MOST TERRIBLE BUT MAGNIFICENT RIDE I EVER TOOK IN MY LIFE.—NINETY MILES ON THE BACK OF A FLYING MASS OF ICE, AND HOW BULGER AND I WERE LANDED AT LAST ON THE BANKS OF A MOST WONDERFUL RIVER.—HOW THE DAY BROKE IN THIS UNDER WORLD.

Had my hand at that moment not grasped a cord tied to the neck of my wise and keen-eyed Bulger, I really believe I would have come to a halt, faced about, retraced my steps, and begged the inhabitants of this crystal realm to admit me once more into the cold kingdom where Gelidus held his icy court; for a sudden fit of depression came upon me as the chilly air struck against my cheeks and I saw the deep darkness made visible by the tiny flame of my alabaster lamp.

Cold though it might be, I would have sunshine in the icy land of the Koltykwerps, but now how could I tell what fate awaited me?

Luckily, I had asked the captain of the meat quarries to allow me to retain one of his sounding-rods with its flint point, for I feared lest in descending some icy declivity I might fall and bruise, or even break, a limb.

I was determined to advance cautiously along this icy passage, shrouded as it was in impenetrable gloom, and so different from the broad and polished pavement of the Marble Highway; and hence, hanging the lamp about my neck, I proceeded to make use of the sounding-rod as an alpenstock, for which purposes it was admirably adapted. Suddenly Bulger halted, gave a low whine of warning, and turned back. In an instant I knew that there was danger ahead, and letting myself drop on my hands and knees crawled carefully along to make an investigation of the dangerous spot in our route signalled by the watchful Bulger.

It was only too true: we stood apparently upon the very edge of a sheer parapet, how high I had no way of ascertaining, but I was unable to reach any bottom with the sounding-rod.

What was to be done? Turn back?

It was not yet too late, the Koltykwerpian quarrymen could not have completed their task in so short a time, they would hear my knock, they would tear down their wall of ice, and Gelidus and Schneeboule would welcome us back to their ice palace with a cold, but honest satisfaction.

As I sat there plunged in thought, I half unconsciously began to twirl the sounding-rod around until I had sunk it half its length into the floor of ice, and then reaching out I encircled Bulger with my arm and drew him up against me as was my wont when preparing for profound meditation.

I had scarcely done so when the ice beneath me gave one of those sharp, clear, cracking noises so unlike the sound made by the breaking of any other substance; and thereupon I felt the crystal mass on which Bulger and I were sitting tremble and vibrate for an instant, and then, with a sudden downward cant, break away from the mass behind it and begin to move!

Instinctively a sense of my awful peril prompted me to cling to the sounding-rod which I had sunk drill-like into the ice. Luckily it was between my legs, and quick as a flash I intwined them around it, assuming a Turkish sitting posture, while my left arm was wrapped tightly around Bulger's body.

I don't know how it was done, done as it was all in an instant; but there I sat now firmly saddled, so to speak, upon that crystal monster's back, as with a creak and a crash it snapped the crystal links which bound it to the wall of ice and plunged headlong down the glassy slope.

In my fright I had dropped my lamp, and now the deep gloom of this under world inwrapped me. But no, it was not so, for as the escaping block of ice creaked and craunched its way along, the two cold crystal surfaces gave forth a weird glimmer of phosphorescent light which made the flying mass seem like a monstrous living thing, out of whose thousand eyes were darting tongues of flame as it rushed madly along, now gaining speed upon striking a steeper stretch of way, now fouling with some obstruction and dashing against the rocky sides of the corridor, and sending a shower of crystals sparkling and glittering in the black air!

Anon the escaping block comes upon a gentle slope, and with the low music of crushing crystals slips softly along in its flight as if mounted upon runners of polished steel, and then with a sudden dip it glides upon a sharper descent and fairly leaps into the air as it bounds along, hissing over the slippery roadway, and leaving a train of fire behind it. And now it strikes a stretch of way piled here and there with clumps and blocks of ice.

With a mad fury it springs upon the lesser ones with a growl of rage, grinding them to powder, which, like showers of icy foam, it hurls upon Bulger and me seated on its back. But some of the blocks resist its terrible onslaught and our mighty steed is hurled from side to side with crash and creak, as it drives its crystal corners fiercely against the jutting rocks, leaving marks of its white flesh on these black heads of adamant.

It seems an hour since the crystal monster broke away, and yet ever downward he threads his wild flight, butting, bumping, jostling, veering, staggering along, bearing Bulger and me to the lowest level of the World within a World.

Will he never end his mad flight?

Is there no way for me to curb him?

Must he fly until he has ground his very body to such a thinness that the next obstruction will shatter it into ten thousand pieces, and hurl Bulger and me to death?

As these thoughts are flitting through my mind, the flying mass takes one last mad plunge which lands it on an almost level stretch of roadway, and by the different sound given out by the sliding block, I know that we have left the regions of ice behind us, and that our crystal sledge is gliding gently along over a track of polished marble.

But, mile after mile, it still glides along, gently, softly, silently, and then I dare to think that our lives are saved.

But so terrible had been the strain, so fearful the anxiety, so exhausting the effort necessary to hold my place on the block of ice, and keep my beloved Bulger from slipping out of my arms, that I fell backward into a dead faint as the gliding mass came, at last, to a standstill. I think I must have lain there a good half hour or so; for when I came to myself Bulger's frantic joy told me that he had been terribly wrought up over me, and the moment I opened my eyes he began to shower caresses on my hands and face in most lover-like style. Dear, grateful heart, he felt that he owed his life this time to his little master, and he wanted me to understand how thankful he was.

The moment Bulger's nerves had recovered from the shock occasioned by my prolonged faint, I reached for my repeater and touched its spring.

It registered one hour and a half since we had stepped through the icy portal of King Gelidus' domain. Allowing a half-hour for the time I lay unconscious, it showed that our mad descent on the back of the crystal monster had lasted quite a full hour, and reckoning the average speed of the escaping mass of ice to have been a mile and a half a minute, that we were now in the neighborhood of ninety miles away from the cold kingdom where Gelidus sat on his icy throne, and Princess Schneeboule at his feet with Chillychops beside her.

It was with great difficulty that I could rise to my feet, so stiffened were my joints and knotted my muscles after that terrible ride, every instant of which I expected to be dashed to pieces against projecting rocks, or torn to shreds by being caught between the fleeing monster of ice and the gigantic icicles hanging from the ceiling like the shining teeth of some huge creature of this under world.

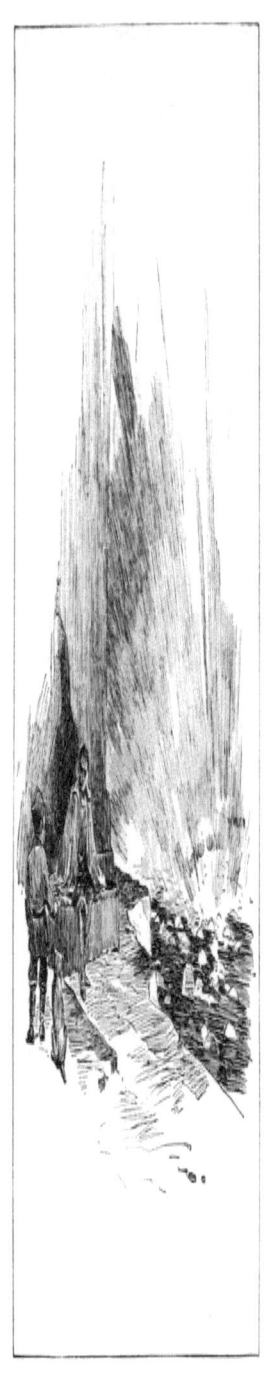

THE TROPICS OF THE UNDER WORLD.

But could it be, dear friends, that Bulger and I had only escaped a quick and merciful ending to be brought face to face with a death ten times more terrible, in that it was to be slow and gradual, denied even the poor boon of looking upon each other, for darkness impenetrable was folded about us and silence so deep that my ears ached in their longing for some sound to break it. And yet there was something in the sound of my own voice that startled me when I used it: it seemed as if the awful stillness were angered at being disturbed by it, and smote it back into my teeth.

Where are we? This was the question I put to myself, and then in my mind I strove to recall every word which I had read in the musty pages of Don Fum's manuscript concerning the World within a World; but I could recollect nothing to enlighten me, not a word to give me hope or cheer, and I was about to cry out in utter despair when, happening to raise my eyes and look off in the distance, I saw what seemed to me to be a jack-a-lantern dancing along on the ground.

It was a strange and fantastic sight in this region of inky darkness, and for a moment I stood watching it with bated breath and wide-opened eyes; but no, it could not be a will-with-the-wisp, for now the faint and uncertain glimmer had increased to a mild but steady glow, reaching away off in the distance like a long line of dying camp-fires seen through an enveloping mist.

But in a moment's time this wide encircling ring of light had so increased in brightness that it looked for all the world like a break o' day in the land o' sunshine, and here and there where its mild effulgence overcame the darkness of this subterranean region, I caught sight of walls and arches and columns of snow-white marble. And then as I called to mind Don Fum's mysterious reference to "sunrise in the lower world," I swung my hat and gave a loud cry of joy, while Bulger waked the echoes of these spacious caverns by his barking. I tell you, dear friends, not until you have been in just such a plight can you know just how such a rescue feels.

And now, no doubt, you are a bit anxious to know what sort of a sunrise could possibly take place in this under world miles below our own.

Well, when you have travelled as many miles as I have, and seen as many wonders as I have, you'll be ready to admit that wonders are quite as commonplace as commonplace itself. Know, then, that this vast region of the World within a World was girt round about by a broad and placid stream whose waters swarmed with vast numbers of gigantic radiate animals, such as polyps, sea-urchins, Portuguese men-of-war, sea-anemones, and the like; that these transparent creatures, which had the power of emitting light, after lying dormant for twelve hours, gradually unfolded their bodies and tentacles, and rose toward the surface of these calm and limpid waters, increasing by degrees their mysterious radiance, until they had chased the darkness from the vast caverns opening upon the banks of the river, and lighted up this under world with a soft effulgence somewhat brighter than the rays of our full moon. For twelve hours these weird lanterns of the stream made it day for this nether world, and then, as they gradually shrank together and sank out of sight, their expiring fires glowed with all the multicolored radiance of our fairest twilight, and the night, blacker than Stygian darkness, came back again. But now 'twas full daylight, and bidding Bulger follow me I walked in silent wonder along the banks of this glowing stream, which, like a band of mysterious fire, as far as my eye could reach went circling around the white marble mouths of these vast underground chambers.

CHAPTER XXXI

IN WHICH YOU READ OF THE GLORIOUS CAVERNS OF WHITE MARBLE FRONTING ON THE WONDERFUL RIVER.—IN THE TROPICS OF THE UNDER WORLD.—HOW WE CAME UPON A SOLITARY WANDERER ON THE BANKS OF THE RIVER.—MY CONVERSATION WITH HIM, AND MY JOY AT FINDING MYSELF IN THE LAND OF THE RATTLEBRAINS, OR HAPPY FORGETTERS.—BRIEF DESCRIPTION OF THEM.

With every turn in the winding way that skirted the white shores of this wonderful stream, its swarms of light-emitting animals lent it a new beauty; for as the day advanced—if I may so express it—they lifted their glowing bodies nearer and nearer to the surface, until now the river shone like molten silver; and as the sheer walls of rock on the opposite bank held set in them vast slabs of mica, the effect was that these gigantic natural mirrors reflected the glowing stream with startling fidelity, and threw the flood of soft light in dazzling shimmer against the fantastic portals of the white marble caverns on this side of the stream. It was a scene never to forget, and again and again I paused in silent wonder to feast my eyes upon some newly discovered beauty. Now, for the first, I noted that every white marble basin of cove and inlet was filled with a different glow, according to the nature of the tiny phosphorescent animals which happened to fill its waters,—one being a delicate pink, another a glorious red, the third a deep rich purple, the fourth a soft blue, the fifth a golden yellow, and so on, the charm of each tint being greatly enhanced by the snowy whiteness of these marble basins, through which long lines of curious fish scaled in hues of polished gold and silver swam slowly along, turning up their glorious sides to catch the full splendor of the light reflected from the mica mirrors. And now the chilly breath of King Gelidus' domain no longer filled the air. I stood in the tropics of the under world, so to speak; and but one thing was lacking to make my enjoyment of this fairy region complete, and that was some one to share it with me.

True, Bulger had an idea of its beauty, for he testified his happiness at being once more in a warm land by executing some mad capers for my amusement, and by scampering along the shore of the glowing river and barking at the stately fish as they slowly fanned the water with their many colored fins; but I must admit that I longed for the Princess Schneeboule to keep me company. But it was a rash wish; for the warm air would have thrown her into convulsions of fear, and she would have preferred to meet her death in the cool river rather than attempt to breathe such a fiery atmosphere. By this time I had advanced several miles along the white shores of the glowing stream, and, feeling somewhat fatigued, I was about to sit down on the jutting edge of a natural bench of rock, which seemed almost placed on the river banks by human hands for human forms to rest upon and watch the wonderful play of tints and hues in this wide sweeping inlet, when, to my amazement, I saw that a human creature was already sitting there.

His eyes were fixed upon the water, and methought that his face, which was gentle and placid, wore a tired look. Certainly he was plunged into such deep meditation that he either took or feigned to take no notice of my approach.

Bulger was inclined to dash forward and attract his attention by a string of earsplitting barks, but I shook my head. This wanderer along the glowing stream of day wore rather a graceful cloak-like garment, woven of some substance that shimmered in the light, and so I concluded that it must be mineral wool. His head was bare, and so were his legs to the knees, his feet being shod with white metal sandals tied on with what looked like leathern thongs. All in all, he had a friendly though somewhat peculiar look about him, and his attitude struck me as being that of a person either plunged into deep thought, or possibly listening for some anxiously expected signal. At any rate, accustomed as I was to meet all sorts of people on my travels in the four corners of the globe, I determined to make bold enough to interrupt the gentleman's meditations and wish him good-morrow.

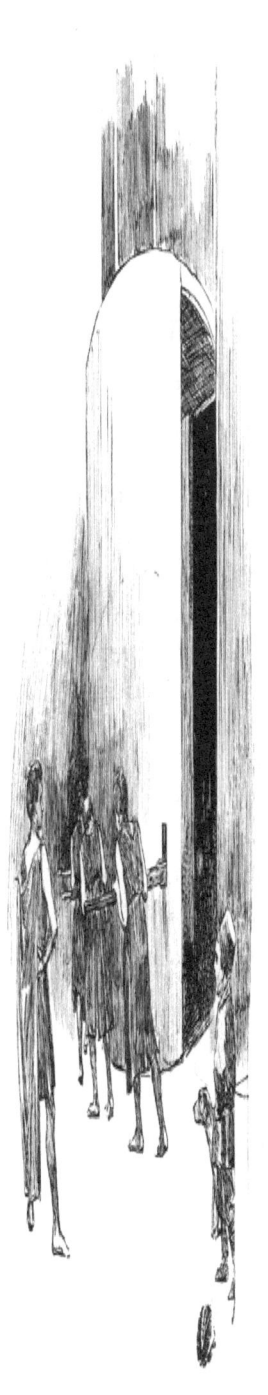

THROUGH THE REVOLVING DOOR.

"Whom have I the pleasure of meeting in this beautiful section of the World within a World?"

The man looked at me in a dazed sort of way and replied,—

"I really don't know, I'm happy to say."

"But, sir, thy name!" I insisted.

"Forgot it years ago," was his remarkable answer.

"But surely, sir," I exclaimed rather testily, "thou art not the sole inhabitant of this beautiful under world,—thou hast kinsman, wife, family?"

"Ay, gentle stranger," he replied in slow and measured tones, "there are people farther along the shore, and they are good, dear souls, although I have forgotten their names, and I have, too, a very faint recollection that two of those people are sons of mine. Stop! no, their names are gone from me too, I forgot them the day my own name slipped from my mind!" and as he uttered these words he threw his head back with a sudden jerk and I heard a strange click inside of it, as if something had slipped from its place, and that instant a mysterious expression used by that Master of Masters, Don Fum, flashed through my mind.

Rattlebrains! Yes, that was it; and now I felt sure that I was standing in the presence of one of the curious folk inhabiting the World within a World, to whom Don Fum had given the strange name of Rattlebrains, or Happy Forgetters.

I was so delighted that I could barely keep myself from rushing up to this gentle-visaged and mild-mannered person, whose head had just given forth the sharp click, and grasping him by the hand. But I feared to shock him by such a friendly greeting, and so I contented myself with crying out,—

"Sir, thou seest before thee none other than the famous traveller, Baron Sebastian von Troomp!" but to my great amazement and greater chagrin he simply turned his strange eyes, with the far-away look, upon me for an instant, and then resumed his contemplation of the beautifully tinted sheet of water, as if I hadn't opened my mouth. It was the most extraordinary treatment that I had experienced since my descent into the under world, and I was upon the point of resenting it, as became a true knight and especially a von Troomp, when Don Fum's brief description of the Rattlebrains, or Happy Forgetters, flitted through my mind.

Said he, "By the exercise of their strong wills they have been busy for ages striving to unload their brains of the to them now useless stock of knowledge accumulated by their ancestors, and the natural consequence has been that the brains of these curious folk, who call themselves the Happy Forgetters, relieved of all labor and strain of thought, have absolutely shrunken rather than increased in size, so that with many of the Happy Forgetters their brains are like the shrivelled kernel of a last year's nut and give forth a sharp click when they move their heads suddenly with a jerk, as is often their wont, for they take great pride in proving to the listener that they deserve the name of Rattlebrain.

"Nor do I need remind thee, O reader," concluded Don Fum, in his celebrated work on the "World within a World," "that the chiefest among the Happy Forgetters is the man whose head gives forth the loudest and sharpest click; for he it is who has forgotten most."

You can have but a faint idea, dear friends, of my delight at the prospect of spending some time among these curious people—people who look with absolute dread upon knowledge as the one thing necessary to get rid of before happiness can enter the human heart.

No joy can equal the Happy Forgetter's when, upon clasping a friend's hand, he finds that he has forgotten his very name; and no day is well spent in this land at the close of which the inhabitant may not exclaim,—

"This day I succeeded in forgetting something that I knew yesterday!"

At last the Happy Forgetter rose from his seat and calmly walked away, without so much as wishing me good-day; but I was resolved not to be so easily gotten rid of, so I called after him in a loud voice, and Bulger, following my example, raised a racket at his heels, whereupon he faced about and remarked,—

"Beg pardon, I had quite forgotten thee, I'm happy to say, and thy name too, I've forgotten that; let me see, Art thou a radiate?" (One of the animals in the water.) I was more than half inclined to lose my temper at this slur, classing me, a back-boned animal, with a mere jelly-fish; but under all the circumstances I thought it best to control myself, for I could well imagine that from the size of my head and the utter absence of all click inside of it, I was not destined to be a very welcome visitor among the Happy Forgetters; and therefore, swallowing my injured feelings, I made a very low bow, and begged this curious gentleman to be kind enough to conduct me to his people—among whom I wished to abide for a few days.

CHAPTER XXXII

HOW WE ENTERED THE LAND OF THE HAPPY FORGETTERS.—SOMETHING MORE ABOUT THESE CURIOUS FOLK.—THEIR DREAD OF BULGER AND ME.—ONLY A STAY OF ONE DAY ACCORDED US.—DESCRIPTION OF THE PLEASANT HOMES OF THE HAPPY FORGETTERS.—THE REVOLVING DOOR THROUGH WHICH BULGER AND I ARE UNCEREMONIOUSLY SET OUTSIDE OF THE DOMAIN OF THE RATTLEBRAINS.—ALL ABOUT THE EXTRAORDINARY THINGS WHICH HAPPENED TO BULGER AND ME THEREAFTER.—ONCE MORE IN THE OPEN AIR OF THE UPPER WORLD, AND THEN HOMEWARD BOUND.

The Happy Forgetter pursued his way calmly along the winding path that skirted the glowing river, apparently, and no doubt really, unconscious of the fact that Bulger and I were following close at his heels. After half an hour or so of this silent tramp, he suddenly came to a standstill, and with his placid countenance turned toward the light seemed to be so far away in thought that for several moments I hesitated to address him. But as there were no signs of his showing any disposition to come to himself, I made bold to ask him the cause of the delay.

"I'm happy to say," he remarked, without so much as deigning to turn his head, "that I've forgotten which of these two roads leads to the homes of our people."

Well, this was a pleasant outlook to be sure, and, I don't know what we should have done had not Bulger solved the difficulty for us by making choice of one of the paths and dashing on ahead with a bark of encouragement for us to follow.

CAUGHT UP IN THE ARMS OF THE TORRENT.

When I assured the Happy Forgetter that he need have no fear as to the wisdom of the choice, he gave a start of almost horror at the information; for you must know, dear friends, that the Happy Forgetter has more dread of knowledge than we have of ignorance. To him it is the mother of all discontent, the source of all unhappiness, the cause of all the dreadful ills that have come upon the world, and the people in it.

"The world," said one of the Happy Forgetters to me sadly, "was perfectly happy once, and man had no name for his brother, and yet he loved him even as the turtle-dove loves his mate, although he has no names to call her by. But, alas, one day this happiness came to an end, for a strange malady broke out among the people. They were seized with a wild desire to invent names for things; even many names for the same thing, and different ways of doing the same thing. This strange passion so grew upon them that they spent their lives in making them in every possible way harder to live. They built different roads to the same place, they made different clothes for different days, and different dishes for different feasts. To each child they gave two, three, and even four different names; and different shoes were fashioned for different feet, and one family was no longer satisfied with one drinking-gourd. Did they stop here?

"Nay, they now busied themselves learning how to make different faces to different friends, covering a frown with a smile, and singing gay songs when their hearts were sad. In a few centuries a brother could no longer read a brother's face, and one-half the world went about wondering what the other half was thinking about; hence arose misunderstandings, quarrels, feuds, warfare. Man was no longer content to dwell with his fellow-man in the spacious caverns which kind nature had hollowed out for him, piercing the mountains with winding passages beside which his narrow streets dwindled to merest pathways."

In the Land of the Happy Forgetters care never comes to trouble sleep, nor anxious thought to wear the dread mask of To-morrow!

Happy the day on which this child of nature might exclaim: "Since morn I've forgotten something! I've unloaded my mind! It's one thought lighter than it was!"

He was the happiest of the Happy Forgetters who could honestly say, I know not thy name, nor when thou wast born, not where thou dwellest, nor who thy kinsmen are; I only know that thou art my brother, and that thou wilt not see me suffer if I should forget to eat, or perish of thirst if I forget to drink, and that thou wilt bid me close my eyes if I should forget that I had laid me down to sleep.

Bulger's and my arrival in the Land of the Happy Forgetters filled the hearts of these curious folk with secret dread. At sight of my large head they all began to tremble like children in the dark stricken with fear of bogy or goblin, and with one voice they refused to permit me to sojourn a single brief half-hour among them; but gradually this sudden terror passed off a bit, and after a council held by a few of the younger men, whose brains as yet completely filled their heads, it was determined that I might bide for another day in their land, but that then the revolving door should be opened, and Bulger and I be thrust outside of their domain.

From what Don Fum had written about the Happy Forgetters, I knew only too well that it would be useless for me to attempt to reverse this decree; so I held my peace, except to thank them for this great favor shown me.

The daylight, if I may call it so, now began to wane, or rather the thousands of light-giving creatures swarming in the river now began to draw in their long tentacles, close their flower-like bodies, and slowly sink to the bottom of the stream. I was quite anxious to see whether the Happy Forgetters would make any attempt to light up their cavernous homes, or whether they would simply creep off to bed and sleep out the long hours of pitchy darkness. To my surprise, I now heard the clicking of flints on all sides, and in a moment or so a thousand or more great candles made of mineral wax with asbestos wicks were lighted, and the great chambers of white marble were soon aglow with these soft and steady flames.

The Happy Forgetters were strictly vegetable eaters, feeding upon the various fungous plants growing in these caverns in great profusion, together with a very nutritious and pleasant tasting jelly made from a hardened gum of vegetable origin which abounded in the crevices of certain rocks. There was still another source of food; namely, the nests of certain shellfish, which they built against the face of the rock, just above the surface of the river. These dissolved in boiling water made an excellent broth, very much like the soup from edible birds' nests.

The clothes worn by the Happy Forgetters were entirely woven from mineral wool, which in these caverns gave a long and strong fibre of astonishing softness. The Rattlebrains were tolerably good metal-workers too, but contented themselves with fashioning only such articles as were actually necessary for daily use. Their beds were stuffed with dried seaweed and lichens, and Bulger and I passed a very comfortable night.

As I was forbidden to speak aloud, to ask a question, or to walk abroad unless in company with one of the selectmen, I was not sorry when the moment came for the revolving door to be opened. The Happy Forgetters had been led to believe that Bulger and I were a thousand times more dangerous than scaly monsters or black-winged vampires, and hence they held themselves aloof from us, the children hiding behind their mothers, and the mothers peering through crack and crevice at us.

The size of my head inspired them with a nameless dread, and even the half-a-dozen of the younger and more courageous drew aside instinctively to let me pass.

For the first time in my life I was an object of horror to my fellow-creatures, but I had no hard thoughts against them! Timid children of nature that they were, to them I was as terrible an object as the torch-armed demon of destruction would be to us were he let loose in one of our fair cities of the upper world.

And now the guard of Happy Forgetters had halted in front of what seemed to me to be a huge cask fashioned of solid marble, and set one-half within the white wall of the cavern to which they had led me. But on second glance I saw that there was a row of square holes around its bulge, like those in the top of a capstan.

The Happy Forgetters now disappeared for a moment, and when they joined me again each bore in hand a metal bar, the end of which he set in one of these holes, and then at a signal from the leader the huge half-circle of marble began to turn noiselessly around, exactly like a capstan. As each man's lever came to the wall, he shifted it to the front again. Suddenly, to my amazement, I saw that the great marble cask was hollow, like a sentry box; and you may judge of my feelings, dear friends, upon being politely requested to step inside.

Did I refuse to obey?

Not I. It would have been useless, for was not the whole tribe of Rattlebrains there to lay hands upon me and thrust me in?

So taking off my hat and making a low bow to the little group of Happy Forgetters, I stepped within the hollow cask and Bulger did the same; but not with so good a grace as his master, for, casting an angry glance at the inhospitable dwellers in these chambers of white marble, he growled and laid bare his teeth to show his contempt for them.

Now the great marble cask began to revolve the other way and in a moment it was back in place again.

I heard several sharp clicks as if a number of huge spring latches had snapped into place, and then all was silent as the tomb, and I had almost said as dark too; but no, I could not say that, for I looked out into a low tunnel which ran past the niche in which Bulger and I were standing, and to my more than wonder it was dimly lighted.

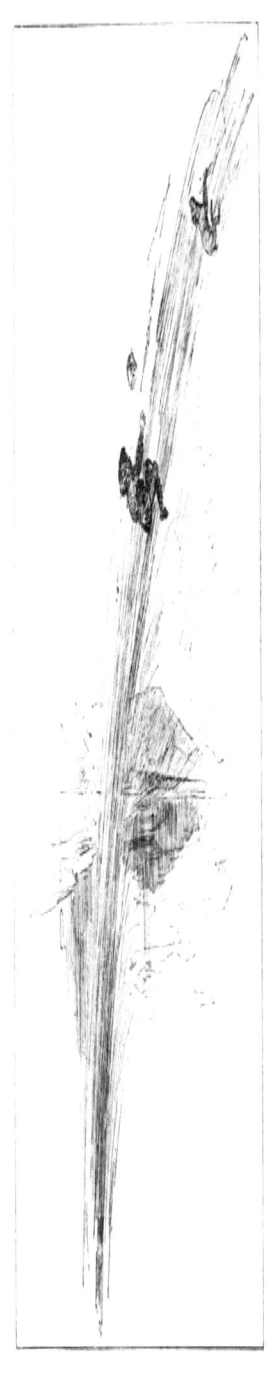

HURLED OUT IN THE SUNSHINE.

I stepped out into it; it was as round as a cannon bore and just high enough for me to stand erect; and now I discovered whence the light proceeded. In the cracks and crevices of its walls grew vast masses of those delicate light-giving fungous rootlets, the glow of which was so strong that I had no difficulty in reading the writing on my tablets; in fact, I stood there for several minutes making entries by the light of these bunches of glowing rootlets.

Then the thought dashed through my mind,—

"Which way shall I turn, to the right or to the left?"

Bulger comprehended the cause of my vacillation and made haste to come to my rescue. After sniffing the air, first in one direction and then in the other, he chose the right hand, and I followed without a thought of questioning his wisdom. Strange to say, he had not advanced more than a few hundred rods before I noticed that there was a strong current of air blowing through the tunnel in the direction Bulger had taken.

Every moment it increased in violence, fairly lifting us from our feet and bearing us along through this narrow bore made by nature's own hands and lighted too by lamps of her own fashioning. The motion of the air through this vast pipe caused bursts of mighty tones as if peeled forth by some gigantic organ played by giant hands. It was strange, but yet I felt no terror as I listened to this unearthly music, although its depth of tone jarred painfully upon my ear-drums.

By the dim light of the luminous rootlets, I could see Bulger just ahead of me, and I was content. No shiver of fear ran down my back, or robbed my limbs of their full power to resist the ever-increasing pressure of the air. But as it grew stronger and stronger, half of my own accord and half because Bulger set the example, I broke into a run. Our pace once quickened it was impossible for me to slow up again. On, on, in a mad race, my feet scarcely touching the bottom of the tunnel, I sped along, while the great pipe through which I was borne on the very wings of the gale sent forth its deep and majestic peal.

There was something strangely and mysteriously exciting in this race, and all that kept me from enjoying it to my full bent was the thought that a sudden increase in the violence of the blast might toss me violently on my face and possibly break an arm for me or injure me in some serious way.

All at once the deep pealing forth of the organ-like tone ceased, and in its stead came the awful sound of rushing water. Before I had time to think, it was upon me, striking me like a terrific blow from some gigantic fist wearing a boxing-glove. The next instant I was caught up like a cork on a mountain torrent, swayed from side to side, twisted, turned, sucked down and cast up again, whirled over and over, tossed and tumbled, rolled along like a wheel, my arms and legs the spokes!

Wonderful to relate, I did not lose consciousness as this terrible current shot me like a stick of timber through a flume, whither I knew not, only that the speed and volume went ever on increasing until at last the tumultuous torrent filled the tunnel, and robbed me of light, of breath, of life, of everything, including my faithful and loving Bulger!

How long it lasted—this fearful ride in the arms of these mad waters, rushing as if for life or death through this narrow bore—I know not; I only know that my ears were suddenly assailed with a mighty whizz and rush of water as through the nozzle of some gigantic hose, and that I was shot out into the glorious sunshine, out into the grand, free, en air of the upper world, and sent flying up toward the far, blue sky with its flecks of fleecy cloudlets, and Bulger some twenty feet ahead of me, and that then, with a gracefully curved flight through the soft and balmy air of harvest time, we both were gently dropped into a quiet little lake nestled at the foot of a hillside yellow with ripened corn. In a moment or so we had swum ashore. Bulger wanted to halt and shake the water from his thick coat, but I couldn't wait for that. Wet as he was, I clasped him to my heart while he showered caresses on me. But not a word was said, not a sound was uttered. We were both of us too happy to speak, and if you have ever been in that state, dear friends, you know how it feels.

I can't describe it to you.

At this moment some men and boys clad in the garb of the Russian peasant came racing across the fields to see what I was about, no doubt, for I had stripped off my heavy outside clothing, and was spreading it out in the sun to dry.

Upon sight of these red-cheeked children of the upper world I was so overcome with joy that for a minute or so I couldn't get a syllable across my lips, but making a great effort I cried out,—

"Fathers! Brothers! Where am I? Speak! dear souls!"

"In north-eastern Siberia, little soul," replied the eldest of the party, "not far from the banks of the Obi; but whence comest thou? By Saint Nicholas, I believe thou wast spit out of the spouting well! What art thou doing here alone?"

I paid no attention to the question. I was thinking of something else of more importance to me, to wit: my splendid achievement, the marvellous underground journey I had just completed, fully five hundred miles in length, passing completely under the Ural Mountains! After a short stay at the nearest village, I engaged the best guide that was to be had, and crossing the Urals by the pass in the most direct line, re-entered Russia and made haste to join the first government train on its way to St. Petersburg.

Having despatched an *avant courier* with letters to my beloved parents, informing them of my good health and whereabouts, I passed several weeks very pleasantly in the Russian capital, and then by easy stages set out for home.

The elder baron came as far as Riga to meet me, and brought me the best of news from Castle Trump, that my dear mother was in perfect health, and that she and every man, woman, and child in and about the castle were anxiously waiting to give me a real German welcome back home again. And here, dear friends, *mit herzlichen Grüsse*, Bulger and I take our leave of you.

End

Made in United States
Troutdale, OR
11/08/2023